Francis David Morice

The Olympian and Pythian odes of Pindar

Francis David Morice

The Olympian and Pythian odes of Pindar

ISBN/EAN: 9783742875389

Manufactured in Europe, USA, Canada, Australia, Japa

Cover: Foto ©Andreas Hilbeck / pixelio.de

Manufactured and distributed by brebook publishing software
(www.brebook.com)

Francis David Morice

The Olympian and Pythian odes of Pindar

THE

OLYMPIAN AND PYTHIAN

ODES OF PINDAR.

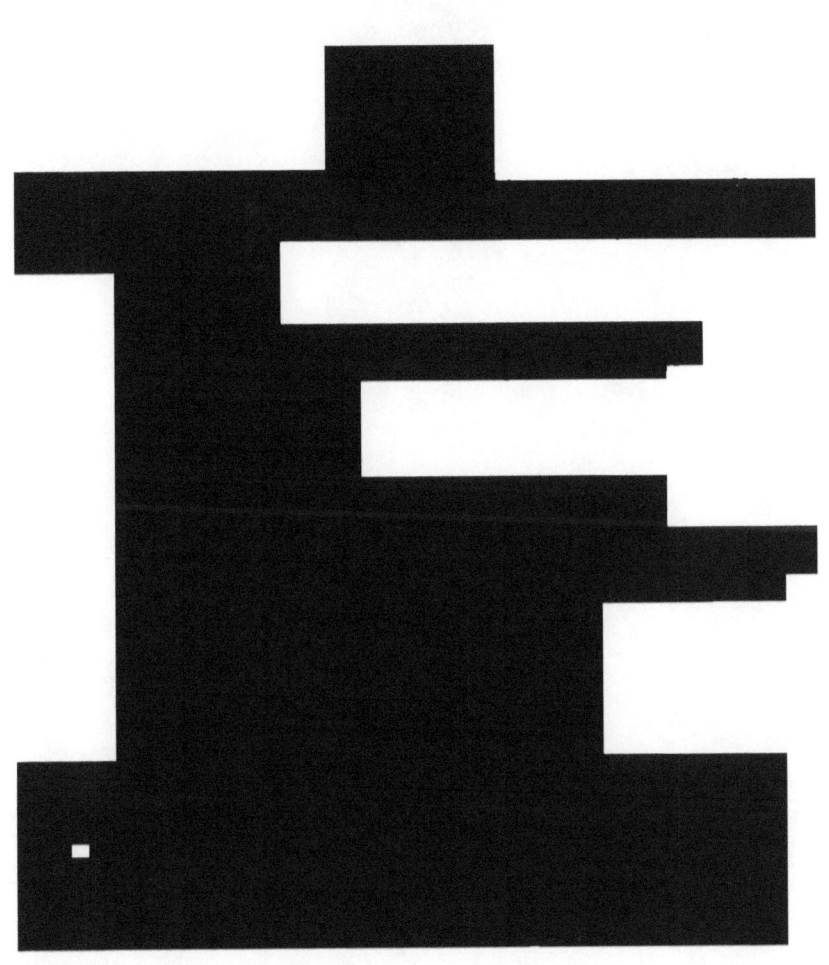

HENRY S. KING & CO., LONDON..

1876.

TRANSLATOR'S PREFACE.

A BRIEF SKETCH of the difficulties attending such a work as the present will perhaps be the best apology for its shortcomings. It is probably needless to dwell on such as are common to all translators : the prefaces of the late Professor Conington and others have practically exhausted that question. Upon such as arise from the special characteristics of my author, a few words hereafter may not be out of place. But there are others for which I am myself responsible ; those, namely, which spring from the ideal of translation at which I have felt bound to aim—an ideal involving severer restrictions than most translators have cared to accept, and consequent labour, which might, under shelter of good precedents, have been evaded. That the present translation does not fully realize this ideal, is only too certain ; but at least I have never consciously abandoned it ; and believing it to be, in spite of all difficulties, true and good in itself, I venture to claim at least the credit of an attempt in the right direction.

A perfect translation should, if I mistake not, set before its readers, not merely all the original author's *substance*, but very much also of his *form*. The diction and metrical shape of a first-rate Greek or Latin poem are scarcely less essential to the effect which it produces as a whole, than the thoughts to which these surroundings have been given. The perfectly natural and harmonious adaptation of form to matter is one of the most striking and special characteristics of the best classical literature. We see it in prose and verse alike. The εἰρομένη λέξις of Herodotus, the Dialogue form of Plato, the 'Antithesis' of early Attic oratory, developing into the Demosthenic 'Period,' are instances which will at once occur to the student of Greek prose literature. And so the poetic form common to, *e.g.*, Homer, Pindar, and Sophocles, together with their several peculiarities of rhythm and diction, are no mere accidental veil, which a translator may strip away without detriment to the thoughts contained in them. Rather they are the external shape in which those thoughts naturally and spontaneously embody themselves, as appropriate to them as a particular foliage to a particular tree. Homer in prose, or Pindar in blank verse, bears to its original much such a relation as a ship's mast to a fir-tree, or a trim-clipped hedge to a wild hawthorn:—the change in form amounts to a change of essence. The old style of translation, which gave a common character of metre and diction to the visions of Hebrew prophets, the songs of prehistoric Grecian bards, and the lucubrations of learned Alexandrians or Roman courtier-poets of the Empire, produced some great poems, and augmented the treasures of English literature; but an intelligent student might read Pope's "Iliad" from end to end without gaining the least insight into the real character of the Homeric writings. The translator who wishes to convey to his readers a true conception of his original, must first solve a problem which is often one of no little difficulty. He must discover or invent for his work such a form as may accord with the canons of English poetry, and so be intelligible to the English reader, yet may at the same time retain all that it is possible to retain of the peculiarities of style and metre which distinguished the original.

Thanks to the labours of comparatively recent writers, some simple metres of Greek and Latin poets are now more or less naturalized in English. The next generation will probably find nothing bizarre or pedantic in an English hexameter version of Homer, or a reproduction of Horace's Odes in their original rhythms. Thus future translators of these authors may find the question of metre solved for them. But the complicated structure of Pindaric verse, in which all kinds of feet are freely blended in a single line, and in which the strophe rather than the line is the real unit of measurement, perplexes, even in the original language, readers whose ear has been tuned by the simple metres of modern poetry. And considering the uncertainty of English quantity and accent, I am persuaded that a reproduction syllable by syllable of Pindar's rhythms would be to most readers simply unintelligible. Long successions of equivalent syllables, such as spondaic and proceleusmatic rhythms require, are practically impossible in English : the whole character of our accentuation requires the emphasizing of some syllables and the slurring of others, with less regard to their natural length or shortness than to a sort of "chiaroscuro" with which no English ear can dispense. No doubt the Poet Laureate, in his striking "Experiment," *Boadicea*, has succeeded in combining at the end of each line very remarkable sequences of quantitatively short syllables. But our habit of accentuation seriously interferes with their actual effect as read. Nine out of every ten Englishmen would certainly pronounce,

"fierce volubility,"

or,

"Druid and Druidess,"

as pairs of dactyls. And where Mr. Tennyson's success is but partial, an ordinary writer may fairly shrink from repeating the attempt. Οὔ μιν διώξω· κεινὸς εἴην !

Deterred by these considerations from a literal reproduction

of Pindaric metres, yet unable to acquiesce in a form which
should wholly ignore them, I have endeavoured to shape for
myself a middle course, not ideally satisfactory, yet the best
which I can devise. I have taken as a basis existing English
metres, but have endeavoured to treat them with such freedom
of combination, and occasional substitution of, *e.g.,* anapaests for
iambics, and dactyls for trochees, as to produce some faint re-
flection of Pindar's ever-shifting rhythm. I have followed my
original,—with no more licence than he allows himself,—in the
exact syllabic agreement of corresponding stanzas. In the con-
struction of each strophe I have taken pains that the proportion
of length between one line and another should, as far as possible,
answer to that observed in the original, any marked contrast between one line and another in this respect being always repro-
duced in the translation, and the original number of lines in a
stanza being invariably retained. In short, I have done my best,
with what success my readers must judge, to grasp the general
rhythmical idea of each ode, and to utilize the materials supplied
by ordinary English metre in such a spirit as that in which
Pindar dealt with the ordinary rhythms of his own day, mingling
them in new combinations, and bringing out by contrasts and
modifications fresh effects from old metrical forms.

The diction of Pindar is exceedingly characteristic, and quite
essential to the general effect of his poetry. I have striven to
give some idea of it by seizing its most salient points, actually
to reproduce it is probably impossible. His audacity of expression verges on the grotesque ; and I fear that a close following of
him has sometimes carried me over the precipice on whose edge
he treads. Yet it has seemed better to run this risk than to
lose so essential a point in his style. Again, his thought is so

rapid, that its transitions bewilder the reader. Metaphor treads on the heels of metaphor. A subject is started, suddenly dropped, and as suddenly resumed. The most unexpected turns are given to the most simple matters. He passes from fact to allegory, and from allegory to fact, within the compass of a single sentence, and without the slightest warning. Thus, in the sixth Olympian, Phintias, the successful charioteer, is invoked to harness his mules,—the mules that conquered at Olympia,—to the imaginary car of Pindar's poetry; and thus, drawn by this compound of fact and fancy,—the real mules and the ideal car,—the poet and the driver are to ride together through the gates of song to Pitane,—birthplace of the victorious family,—*who* (!) (for the place is here suddenly personified, or rather identified with its eponymous Nymph) was bride of Poseidon, and mother of Evadne. Whereupon the story passes to the adventures of this Evadne, and Phintias and his mules drop once more out of sight. In all this I have felt bound to follow my original step by step; for, after all, the resulting obscurity is Pindar's own, and it seems to me no part of a translator's duty to make his work more easily intelligible than that of his original. Between Pindar and his English readers, there hang, so to speak, many veils: a foreign language, an unwonted diction, a different way of looking at things, a constant and familiar allusion to forgotten ideas and legends, all tend to obscure his poetry. Of these veils, as I have called them, a translator has, I think, to remove the first alone; the removal of the others is the province of the commentator, the critic, and the literary historian.

These qualities of daring and versatility are attended in Pindar by a kind of sententiousness which is exceedingly unlike anything in ordinary modern writers, and which is consequently hard to reproduce with good effect. He pauses, for example, in a narrative, or an apostrophe, to utter little general maxims and aphorisms, whose very simplicity makes them seem the more oracular. The story of Ixion is interrupted by the obvious remark that a man should observe the limits of his proper sphere; of Tantalus and Pelops—that gods should not be accused of gluttony, and that slander is an unprofitable trade; of Clytemnestra and Agamemnon—that unfaithfulness in a young bride is a public scandal. Quaint as this habit seems to a modern reader, Pindar's little apophthegms have an air of earnestness and simplicity that at once disarms criticism. They seem to spring from him involuntarily, to be the expression of thoughts which are forced on him by the reflex effect of his own words, and of which he must disburden his mind before he can go further. But to an English reader they must always seem odd and unnatural, and as such are cruel stumbling-blocks to the translator, who is compelled to choose between shirking them or boldly reproducing them at the risk of seeming ridiculous. My view of a translator's duty leaves me no such alternative: to omit or disguise them would be a mutilation of my original. *Malo errare cum Pindaro!*

Another prominent feature in Pindar's style, is a certain archaic elevation of tone, which enables him to give dignity to the most trivial thought or circumstance. It requires the nicest caution to preserve this characteristic in a translation without degenerating into bombast and bathos. The style must be kept at a high pitch, yet must avoid the "'Ercles vein," the vocabulary must be antique yet not pedantic, the phrases dignified yet not pompous. The necessity of all this has been constantly and clearly before my eyes; but unfortunately, to see is one thing, to carry out in practice is another. At least, however, where I have failed, my failure has not been due to want of thought or want of pains. I have re-written again and again many awkward passages, till I have either hesitatingly satisfied myself, or reluctantly acquiesced in the necessity of failure.

Before concluding, I ought perhaps to offer a few words in explanation of a comparatively trifling matter. A certain class of scholars will probably take exception to my spelling of Greek proper names. I have written " Hiero " and not " Hieron," " Cassandra " and not " Kassandra," and so forth. On the other hand, I have not latinized " Deinomenes " into " Dinomenes," or " Poseidon " into " Posidon." No doubt this may be called inconsistency; yet I think it is defensible. *Ceteris paribus,* the more accurate transliteration is no doubt preferable to the less; but unfortunately it often results in combinations of letters which are so unfamiliar to English eyes as to be positively repulsive. I cannot bring myself to write " Klutaimnestra," or " Kupris," or " Aias;" each involves the juxtaposition of letters which in English words are, I believe, never found together. In such cases the Latin form of the names offers a welcome escape from a difficulty. Again, the more precise method is not free from dangers of its own. A most eminent scholar and poet has been led by it into the amazing solecism of writing " Peirai*os* " as an improvement on the ordinary " Pirae*us* " (in Greek, Πειραιεύς). " *Incidit in Scyllam, qui vult vitare Charybdim,*" and in this case Charybdis is certainly the lesser evil. But further it may be reasonably doubted whether the extreme importance which is now attached in some quarters to this question of transliteration, does not point to a growing spirit of that worst of all pedantries, pedantry in trifles. If so, a protest against it may sometimes be almost a duty. This plea might perhaps be used to defend the occasional use in this translation of the name "Jove" as a substitute for "Zeus;" but I fear I must, in this case, be truthful enough to own, that no more exalted consideration than the want of a convenient rhyme has induced me to admit it.*

The text followed in this translation is that of Dissen, as edited in 1843 by Schneidewin. Usually also his interpretation has been followed, though in some doubtful places I have exercised the right of private judgment. Other editions have of course been also consulted, but I have rarely found them to shake my confidence in Dissen. Of such previous translations as have come in my way, I have found A. Moore's metrical version incomparably the best, both in scholarship and in literary power. Mr. Myers' recent prose version was unfortunately not published till my own translation was nearly completed, and I have therefore been unable to avail myself of its assistance. Finally, I wish to acknowledge with the sincerest gratitude the help afforded me by my friend and colleague Mr. R. Whitelaw, a former Fellow of Trinity College, Cambridge, who has assisted me in a final revision of the entire work, and enabled me to remove many defects of taste and inaccuracies of rendering, which would otherwise have escaped my notice.

---

* Once or twice, also, I have used such shortened forms as "Thrasybule" for "Thrasybulus;" rather unwillingly, though there is good precedent for the practice.

CONTENTS.

PINDAR'S ODES.

OLYMP. I.

TO HIERO, KING OF SYRACUSE, VICTOR IN THE HORSE-RACE.

STROPHE.

PEERLESS is water.   Gold, like flames that gleam
   In darkest night, doth proudest wealth outshine.
But oh ! if contests be the theme
   Thou choosest, heart of mine !
      As soon expect some star more fair
      Shall yon bright sun outblaze in barren air,
As hope of sports to tell, Whose glories may excel
      Olympia, whence harmonious voices spring,
      That fire poetic souls to sing
The son of Cronus, when they come   10
To Hiero's proud and happy home.   .

ANTISTROPHE.

With rod of righteousness the fields he sways
   Of pastoral Sicily, and culls the prime

Of virtue, while around him blaze
    The brightest flowers of rhyme,
        Such festal lays as oft we wake
        Around his board. The Dorian lyre come take !
If haply Pisa's meed, That graced that victor-steed,
        Bright dreams of rapture o'er your spirit shed,
        As by Alpheüs' banks he sped.   20
No need of spur—on, on he flies !
And bears his master toward the prize.

EPODE.

The lord of Syracuse, whose coursers' fame
Shines in the land where Lydian Pelops came,
    New home to found—Pelops, of ocean's king,
Poseidon, loved—whom Clotho drew From out the laver's cleansing dew
    With ivory shoulder glistening.
Marvels are many; yet still stranger tale,
With falsehood tricked, may oft o'er truth prevail.

STROPHE.

Favour, (to whom all earthly joys are due,)   30
    Brings credence oft, and well such art she plies
As makes the truthless tale seem true.
    But wiser faith relies

On evidence of coming days.

Yet errs the mortal least that speaks in praise

Of Gods,—and newly thus, O son of Tantalus,

I'll frame thy tale. What time on Sipylus' height

Thy sire Heaven's favour did requite,

And called the Gods about his board ;

Seized wert thou of the Trident's lord.   40

ANTISTROPHE.

Inspired with love, he bore thee far away,

On shining steeds, to Zeus' exalted home :

Where, even so, in later day

Did Ganymedes come

To Zeus. And when no search might track

Thy flight, nor bring thee to thy mother back ;

Some jealous neighbour's tongue A dark surmise outflung,

And told how, at the caldron's boiling point,

With steel they cleft thee joint from joint,

Then round the board in portions spread   50

The seething flesh, and on thee fed !

EPODE.

I cannot tax blest Powers with greed so gross,—

I dare not ! Oft is slander's gain but loss.

And sure, if e'er Olympian watchers loved

A mortal, Tantalus was blest : Yet ill might he such bliss digest,
　　So pride's excess his ruin proved.
A massy stone did Zeus above him poise,
To threaten aye his head, and banish joys.

STROPHE.

And thus he dwells, doomed with the toiling Three
　　To hopeless pain ; for, from immortals riven,　　　　　　　60
Ambrosia and nectar he
　　To mortal guests had given,
　　　　Whence deathless life himself had won.
　　　　But whoso hopes his daring crimes may shun
The sight of Heaven, is vain ; And so the Gods again
　　　　Sent back his son to join Man's fleeting race.
　　　　And when the dark down fringed his face,
In earliest manhood's blossom-tide,
He duly sought a noble bride,

ANTISTROPHE.

Hippodamia, her Pisan father's boast !　　　　　　　　　　70
　　So to the Lord of ocean's roar he prayed
At midnight on the lone sea-coast.
　　At once, his friend to aid,
　　　　He saw the Trident-armed appear :
　　　　And, " If," he cried, " our love hath made me dear,

"Poseidon, to thy heart; Oh, stay Oenomaus' dart!
　"To Elis bear me in thy car apace,
　"And make me victor in the race.
"For thirteen suitors he hath slain,
"His daughter's wedding to restrain.　　　　　　　80

EPODE.

"Yet direst perils bravest hearts befit.
"Die must we all—then why in darkness sit,
　"Chewing the cud of eld, unknown to fame,
"Stranger to all that graces life? No! set am I to dare the strife;
　"Fulfil thou then my cherished aim!"
He spake, nor vainly prayed: Poseidon gave
His golden car, and wingèd coursers brave.

STROPHE.

Oenomaus fell—and fell the maiden too,
　The victor's prize! Six royal sons she bare
To virtue dear; and now, with due　　　　　　　90
　　Of sacrifices fair,
　　　　He rests beside Alpheüs' wave,
　　　　Hard by yon shrine, whose votaries throng his grave!
　　And through Olympia's ring, The hero's glories fling
　　　　Their beams afar; where rivals swift of feet,
　　　　And deeds of hardiest prowess meet,

And he, that conquers in the strife,
Wins sweetest peace for all his life,

ANTISTROPHE.

Far as may triumphs bless : for nought so high
    As bliss renewed through every changing day.   100
But now the victor-chief must I
    Crown with Aeolian lay,—
        Chivalrous strain ! And well I wot, that ne'er
        Shall living man, renowned for wisdom fair—
As he—and prowess bold, In song's bright coil be told.
        Thy patron deity, my Hiero, still
        Labours to grant thee all thy will :
And, save he quit his post ere long,
I trust with yet a sweeter song

EPODE.

Thy rapid car to greet, and trace aright   110
Song's helpful path to Cronium's sunny height.
    Mine are the boldest shafts the Muses lend
In divers fashions men are great, But highest soars the kingly state,
    No further man may gaze.
Tread thou such heights ! And be it mine to dwell
Mid victors, and in song all Greeks excel !

OLYMP. II.

TO THERO OF ACRAGAS, VICTOR IN THE CHARIOT-RACE.

STROPHE.

HYMNS, whose rule the lyre obeys!
God, hero, man,—whom choose we now for praise?
Of Zeus is Pisa; of Heracles, Firstfruits of his victories,
Olympia's contests spring;
And Thero and his conquering cars we sing,
The generous host, the prop of Acragas,
The last best blossom of a famous race.

ANTISTROPHE.

Long their souls were tried with woes,
Ere by the river-side their blest homes rose,
The pride of Sicily: thenceforth fate With wealth and glory crowned
their state, 10
Their native worth to raise.
May Cronus' son, that high Olympus sways,
Lord of the contests by Alpheus, deign
To hear our prayer, and bring them home again!

This for their sons we ask :— for, what is gone,

(Came it of right or maugre right,) is none,—

    No ! not Time's self, that brought it,—can reverse !

Yet all may be forgot in happier hours ;

    For blessings new destroy the primal curse,

And crush its rebel powers,   20

    When again Heaven's will shall rear

    Wealth's soaring fabric skyward. So we hear

Of Cadmus' daughters and all their woes, How yet more mighty

        blessings rose,

    And triumphed o'er their pain.

Mid heavenly Powers lives now the Lightning-slain,

      Fair Semele. Her Pallas and great Jove

      And He her son, the ivy-crowned, still love.

    And in ocean's depths, they say,

    With Nereus' daughters Ino dwells alway,

In life undying ordained of fate. Ah! ne'er may mortal antedate 30

    The term when life shall cease,

    Nor look, through glad years, to One day of peace—

      His Sun's last child ! But ever to and fro

      The tides of joy and grief athwart us flow.

EPODE.

So too with these. The fortune of their line
Holds them still happy, yet their bliss divine
   Mingles at times with woe, that fleets as fast :
Since Laius met his fatal son, and fell
   Slain in the road, and so came true at last
The Pythian oracle.   40

STROPHE.

   Soon Erinys, keen of sight,
   Slew that fierce house in fratricidal fight.
They fell : yet Polynices slain In famed Thersander lived again,
   Athlete and warrior he,
   Scion and stay of the Adrastidae.
      And sprung of these, Aenesidamus' son
      The meed of lyric praise in right hath won.

ANTISTROPHE.

   Graced himself with Pisa's crown,
   He glories in a brother's like renown,
At Pytho and Corinth whose coursers four, Round the great ring
           sped twelve times o'er   50
   Triumphant. Thus to gain
   The prize we toil for breaks the bonds of pain.
      What cannot wealth in radiant virtues drest,
      That thrills with eager zeal the inmost breast ?

EPODE.

Like some bright star, its glorious beams it throws :
And, blest therewith,—(none better,) Thero knows
    How swiftest vengeance waits the guilty dead
And for the sins men sin in realms of day,
    'Neath earth a stern judge speaks the sentence dread
Of fate's resistless sway.   60

STROPHE.

    But, by day alike and night,
    Upon the righteous rises ever light.
They dwell in a life unvexed of toil, Nor need to task the weary soil,
    Nor waters of the main,
    For scant subsistence.   Tearless days they gain,
        With those Heaven-honoured ones in Truth that joy ;
        While sinners cower 'neath weight of dire annoy.

ANTISTROPHE.

    Happiest they that thrice endure
    Through life and death, and still from sin are pure.
For such Zeus leads to Cronus' tower, Where round about the island
           bower   70
    Of blessed spirits strays
    Breath of sea airs, and golden flowerets blaze,
        Some on fair trees, some of the waters bred :
        Wherewith themselves they garland hands and head.

EPODE.

So Rhadamanthus' just decree ordains,
Assessor meet of Cronus, Him that reigns
    The spouse of Rhea throned all powers above.
Peleus with these, and Cadmus dwells. And there
    His mother brought Achilles, when great Jove
Had melted at her prayer.   80

STROPHE.

    His the might that overthrew
Hector, Troy's pillar stout : and Cycnus slew,
And Morning's Aethiopic son.—Oh, mine are keen shafts, many a one
    Within the quiver stored ;
Of meaning to the wise, but to the horde
        Dark riddles ! much, self-taught, the poet knows,
        But vain their lore, base pair, that croak like crows

ANTISTROPHE.

    Round the heavenly bird of Jove !
Now point the bow ! now, not in war but love,
Speed, soul, the stingless shafts of fame ! And what the mark
        whereat we aim,   90
    But Acragas ? for I
Shall soothly swear, (nor deem the vaunt a lie !)
        Than Thero's, in a hundred years, no land
        Shall rear you kinder heart nor freer hand !

EPODE.

Though envy strive his glories to deface,
(No generous foe, but nursed in natures base,)
    That loves to talk the good man's praise away ;
Yet, as the sand still foils the reckoner's count,
    Such are the joys we owe him. Who shall say
How boundless their amount?   100

OLYMP. III.

ON THE SAME VICTORY AS THE PRECEDING. A HYMN FOR THE FEAST OF THE DIOSCURI AT ACRAGAS.

STROPHE.

MAY Tyndarus' sons so kind to the guest, And lovely Helen, the golden-
tressed,
Joy, as Acragas I greet
With triumph-songs for Thero's coursers fleet,
And, Muse-inspired, in numbers fresh and bright
Festal song and Doric step unite.

ANTISTROPHE.

Such service divine at the poet's hand The conqueror's crownèd lock
demand :
Lyre and flute and shapely lays
Must join Aenesidamus' son to praise
With honour meet. And Pisa bids me sing,
Whence immortal lays for mortals spring :   10

EPODE.

When, in the rites ordained of Heracles,
    The Aetolian arbiter with sentence fair
    Garlands with olive grey the victor's hair!
From Ister's shady fount of yore Amphitryon's son that olive bore,
    Bright guerdon of Olympic victories.

⋅ STROPHE.

He won in peace from the tribes that wait On Phoebus, the Hyper-
        borean state,
    Plants for Zeus' frequented glade,
    To crown the victors, and the concourse shade.
A moon had waxed to perfect orb of fire,
Since he raised the altars of his Sire :   20

ANTISTROPHE.

Already, by rocky Alpheüs' side, To glorious contests sanctified
    Those quinquennial lists were set :—
    And Cronian Pelops' dells were treeless yet!
All naked to the scorching sun they lay :
So to Ister's shores he took his way.

EPODE.

There Leto's child had welcomed him, when he
 Came from the rifted, jagged Arcadian hill,
 Doomed of his Sire at harsh Eurystheus' will
To bring the doe with horns of gold, In mystic recompense of old
 Paid to Orthosia by Taÿgete.   30

STROPHE.

Thus as he came, on his quarry's track, To lands that lie at the
   Northwind's back,
 Rapt he viewed their wondrous trees,
 And longing seized his soul to deck with these
His twelvefold course. Thither, the feast to grace,
Comes he now with Leda's Twins apace !

ANTISTROPHE.

For these he left, when he passed to the sky, To rule his glorious
   sports, where vie
 Rapid cars and feats of might.
 Set is my soul, the glories to recite
By Tyndarus' sons on Thero's house outpoured,
Still that in their honour spreads the board,   40

EPODE.

And serves their godhead still with piety !
   But sure as water knows no peer, and best
   Is gold of riches, Thero's deeds have pressed
To fame's last cape ! What further lies, Is barred alike to fools and
      wise :—
   I will not venture there, else vain were I !

OLYMP. IV.

TO PSAUMIS OF CAMARINA, VICTOR IN THE RACE OF MULE-CARS.

STROPHE.

MIGHTIEST Zeus, of whom is driven   The tireless speed of the burn-
      ing levin ;
Lo ! in its cycle thy feast again Brings me with many a sounding strain,
      These exalted sports to tell.
Swift are the true of heart to greet With smiling face the tidings sweet
      Of friends that prosper well.
      O Lord of Aetna, O Cronus' son !
Lord of the wind-swept piles, that hide Hundred-headed Typho's pride !
Give ear to the lays Our revellers raise,
      For victory's sake at Olympia won.

ANTISTROPHE.

Long shall the hero's glories gleam, For Psaumis' cars are the
      revellers' theme.   10
Crowned with the olive at Pisa won, Eagerly ever he presses on,
      Raising Camarina's fame.

                        C

Heaven henceforth grant his every prayer ! For first, the steeds he
          rears with care,
      Our loftiest praises claim ;
      And his halls have a welcome for every guest ;
And set is his soul with thought sincere, To bless with peace his city dear.
No falsehood shall stain My speech's strain,—
      Experience still is the true man's test.

EPODE.

And the son of Clymenus,
      Once, among the Lemnian dames,   20
Baffled scornful slander thus.
      For when he triumphed in the mailèd games,
Stepping forth the crown to take,
To Hypsipyle he spake :—
      " Such is my speed ! And know,
      " My hands too, and heart are so !
" On heads that have not passed their prime,
      " Locks of grey full often grow,
" Ere the appointed time ! "

OLYMP. V.

*ON THE SAME VICTORY AS THE PRECEDING. A PROCES-
SIONAL HYMN SUNG AT CAMARINA ON PSAUMIS' RETURN.*

STROPHE.

On the proud Olympian pageant, high desert in victor's crown,
  Smile, O daughter of the Ocean ! Deign a welcome to the gift,
  Hither that the victor Psaumis brings thee for his mule-car swift !

ANTISTROPHE.

Glory great, O Camarina, brought he to thy peopled town ;—
  Six twin altars duly decking at the festival most high,
  Where, mid sacrifice of oxen, in the five-days' contests vie

EPODE.

Car, and mule, and rapid courser ; and his triumph brought thee fame,
For thy new town's praises mingled with his father Acro's name.

STROPHE.

As from that loved land of Pelops and Oenomaus he returns,
  Pallas, guardian of the city ! of thy hallowed grove he tells,   10
  Of the river of Oänis, and the lake whereby he dwells,

ANTISTROPHE.

And of Hipparis, that waters all thy host with honoured urns,
 Gathering a stately forest round his banks of storied homes,—
 Guided of whose grace thy people fast from dearth to glory comes !

EPODE.

Toil and lavish hand must labour ever for the glorious prize
Lapped in danger, but its winner shall his townsmen own for wise !

STROPHE.

Zeus, Protector, cloud-throned monarch, ruling on thy Cronian hill,—
 Thou, whose presence crowns Alpheüs' tide, and Ida's reverend cave !
 Unto thee with Lydian flutings come I now, thy grace to crave.

ANTISTROPHE.

With a race of famous heroes may this city flourish still ; 20
 And our great Olympian champion still in happy eld live on,
 In his Poseidonian coursers joying, till his days be done,

EPODE.

Girt about with sons ! Who waters with such dews his happy lot,—
Filled with wealth, and crowned with glory,—godhead's self need
  covet not !

OLYMP. VI.

*TO AGESIAS OF SYRACUSE, A DESCENDANT OF THE HERO
IAMUS, VICTOR IN THE RACE OF MULE-CARS.*

STROPHE.

As who would frame some gorgeous hall, Uprears its porch with
      shapely wall
   On golden pillars hung :
Our song's proud front must glitter from afar.
    Suppose a champion at Olympia crowned,
And patron of Zeus' shine oracular,
    And of famed Syracuse joint-founder owned,—
      Say, how should such lack praise from generous tongue ?

ANTISTROPHE.

Sostratus' son, thy feet around Such sandal fair hath fortune bound !
    Ne'er, save by peril, worth
Won fame in hollow ship, or armèd host :   10
    But prosperous toils remembrance aye awake.
And thee, Agesias, fits that truthful boast,
    Adrastus of Amphiaraus spake,
      When with his steeds the seer was lapt in earth !

EPODE.

Soon as on seven-fold pyre the corpses had sunk in flame,
  Spake in Thebes Talaion's son, " I mourn my army's pride,
" Warrior both and seer !" Nor lesser praise may claim
  Syracuse's hero-child, this glad procession's guide.
No wrangler am I, on striving intent :
  Yet loudly I'll swear, Such truth to declare   20
Unflinching, and the Muses sweet assent !

STROPHE.

Haste, Phintis, yoke thy mules so strong ! For I the soaring car of song
      Through paths untrod must guide
Far back to that heroic house's source.
    And who so well should bear us on our way,
As these that triumphed in Olympia's course ?
    Unbar Song's gates ! for I must come this day
      To Pitane along Eurotas' tide !

ANTISTROPHE.

'Twas she that to Poseidon bare Evadne, such the tale, with hair
      Dark as the violet's hue.   .   30
And when her months of secret pain were done,
    Her trusty retinue the mother bade
Convey the babe to Eilatus' great son,
    That by Alpheüs' side Phaesane swayed.
      Woman, and bride of Phoebus, there she grew !

EPODE.

Vainly from Aepytus hid she the fruits of celestial love.

    Forth, with rage and grief at heart, to Pytho speeding fast,

Counsel he sought of Heaven, that might such woes remove.

    Crimson zone aside the while and silver urn she cast,

And bare in the azure thicket a child   40

    Of heavenly thought : While Loxias brought,

To aid her, Fates, and Ilithyia mild.

STROPHE.

In joy and sorrow mingling thus, To light she brought her Iamus,

    And left him laid on earth.

But thither lo ! with honey's harmless bane

    To feed him, came two heaven-sent bright-eyed snakes :

Homeward from Pytho speeds the king again,

    And question for Evadne's babe he makes,

      " To Phoebus self," he cried, " it owes its birth.

ANTISTROPHE.

" A prophet, destined to excel All mortal men on earth that dwell, 50

    "His fame shall perish ne'er !"

He spake,—but who might hope to find a child,

    Left five days long, alive ? Yet there he lay,

Safe couched in reeds amid the trackless wild,

    His soft limbs bathed in gold and purple ray

      Of violets. So the mother bade him bear

EPODE.

Ever the violets' name.* But in ripening manhood's spring,
   Mid Alpheus' deeps he called on Him that rules the sea,
Sire of his race ! and eke the Delian archer king :
   Praying that some peopled state his care and pride might be. 60
And lo ! from the midnight heaven's dark dome
   His father replies, " Son mine, come, arise !
" My voice shall lead you to a populous home."

STROPHE.

So to the lofty land they came, Where Cronium's sunlit summits flame.
     There won he twofold crop
Of seership,—that unerring voice to hear
   At once ; and, (when the pride of Alcaid line
Should found thronged feast, and strife that knows not peer,
   In ritual honour of his Sire divine,)
     An oracle upon the altar's top.   70

ANTISTROPHE.

And Iamids were men of fame In Greece thenceforth. Then riches came :
     They trod the paths of light,
Revering virtue. Deeds are man's sole test !
   Then what though envy's sneer o'er those impends,
That foremost through the twelvefold course have pressed,

---

* *i.e.* She named him Iamus (Gr. ἴον = violet).

And won the grace that blushing Victory lends?
    Oh, if, Agesias, thy sires aright

EPODE.

Honoured in homes Cyllenian, with off'rings of votive fire,
    Hermes, pursuivant of Gods, o'er sport and strife that reigns,
Arcady's lord! 'Tis he, that with his thundrous Sire   80
    Ever, son of Sostratus, thy happy lot ordains.
Meseemeth a whetstone shrills at my tongue!
    With welcome it rides O'er melody's tides—
My mother's mother bright, Stymphalus-sprung!

STROPHE.

Metope she, that Thebe bare, Equestrian nymph, whose waters fair
    I drink; and, drinking, twine
Bright lays for warriors! First to Here's fame,
    The queen of virgins, stir thy comrades now :—
'Scape we not, Aeneas,* our ancient shame,
    "*Boeotian swine?*" True missive-staff art thou   90
    Of fair-haired Muses, bowl for Song's choice wine!

ANTISTROPHE.

And bid them chant Ortygia' praise, And Syracuse, that Hiero sways
    With rod of righteousness :

---

* Aeneas was to convey this Ode to Agesias, and superintend its public performance.

And bows him to Demeter's rosy feet,
    And her equestrian child, and Zeus whose might
Sways Aetna's hilL Him song and harpings sweet
    Know well ! May he, mid bliss no time can blight,
        Agesias' triumph-train with welcome bless :

EPODE.

Home from a home * that hastens returned from Stymphalus' wall,
    Rich Arcadia's mother-town. 'Twere well on stormy night   100
Over the swift ship's side were anchors twain let fall.
    Heaven to either folk be kind, and make their future bright !
O husband of her whose distaff is gold !
    Grant, God of the seas, Fair journey to these ;—
And bid my songs new blooms of grace unfold !

---

  * Agesias was a citizen both of Syracuse and of Stymphalus. This explains also the next sentence.

OLYMP. VII.

TO DIAGORAS OF RHODES, VICTOR IN THE BOXING-MATCH.

STROPHE.

As some wealthy lord in greeting of his daughter's spouse should lift
In his hand a brimming beaker, where the grape's bright juices
foam,
Passing to the youth a gift,
Erst the crown of all his riches, destined now to other home,
For the honour of his banquet, pleased his new-made son to make
Envied of each friendly feaster for his happy wedlock's sake:

ANTISTROPHE.

So to champions crowned at Pytho and Olympia I send
Draughts of nectar sweet, the Muses' boon, the soul's delicious
fruit,
Gladdening each victor-friend !
Happiest he, that standeth ever girt about with good repute . 10
Now to one and now to other comes the charmer of man's life,
Victory,—with tuneful harpings and the ever-varying fife.

EPODE.

Now, while both are round me breathing, with Diagoras I guide
Poesy's bark to Rhodes' fair isle, to Venus' child and Phoebus' bride.
    There the hero, crowned beside Alpheus and Castalia's spring,
    For his prowess in the ring
    Claims my praises, and Damagetus his sire to Justice dear,
In the isle of three fair cities, near the cape of Asia wide,
    Dwelling, ringed with many an Argive spear !

STROPHE.

Of Tlepolemus their father, and their nation's source, aright   20
    Shall my willing tongue discover truth too long in error lost.
Race were they of sovereign might,—
    Sprung of Heracles, a lineage in their father's right they boast
Zeus-descended, and a mother of Amyntor's ancient clan.
Yet, alas, the snares of evil clog the fairest hopes of man !

ANTISTROPHE.

Nought we know that still to mortals first and last shall prove a good.
    And Alcmena's base-born brother did this nation's founder thus
Smite with staff of olive-wood,
'   Fired with sudden wrath in Tiryns dead he smote Licymnius
Issuing from Midea's chamber,—thus aside doth passion turn   30
Wisest souls,—and forth the slayer sped the will of Heaven to learn.

EPODE.

From the perfumed shrine's recesses came the fair-haired God's reply,
Bidding him from Lerne's headland to a sea-girt home to hie :
To a land, of Heaven's high monarch watered erst with showers
of gold,
When Hephaestus' art of old
Brought with brazen axe Athene from her Father's brow to birth,
And the warrior-maid upspringing shrilled afar a joyous cry,
Startling highest Heaven and mother Earth.

STROPHE.

Then Hyperion's son, whose godhead lightens every child of clay,
Gave commandment that thereafter evermore his offspring dear 40
Solemn sacrifice should pay
To the Goddess, and in splendour high her earliest altar rear,
For the thunder-darting maiden, and her mighty Sire's delight !
Prescient reverence to mortals bringeth ever joy and might :—

ANTISTROPHE.

Yet are times when round us gather shadows of oblivion blind,
And with secret step advancing steal the course of wisdom taught
From remembrance of the mind.
So with these, for thither never seed of radiant flame they brought ;
Void of fire a shrine they hallowed in their city's topmost hold.
Yet rained Zeus upon their people plenteous showers of gleaming gold. 50

EPODE.

And Athene made them matchless in the works of human skill :
Shapes exact of beasts and reptiles all their city's ways did fill.
    Great their glory,—guileless cunning with the prudent aye prevails !
    But 'tis said in ancient tales,
    Not as yet, when Earth was portioned forth of Zeus and Powers
        divine,
Towered the Rhodian isle conspicuous over Ocean's waves, but still
    Deep it lay beneath the whelming brine.

STROPHE.

None was there to claim a portion for the absent God of Light,
    Him, the pure and holy One, they left disfranchised of his lot.
Wherefore, when he urged his right,   60
    Zeus ordained a fresh allotment : but such course he suffered not,
For he said he saw a country rising from the hoary deep,
Rich in sustenance for man and plenteous pasturage for sheep.

ANTISTROPHE.

Straight to Lachesis with coronal of gold he made his prayer,
    That, with hands on high uplifted, to the Gods' exalted vow
She no feigned assent should swear,
    But with Cronus' son should grant him for a crown to grace his brow,
When to light should rise such country, he its future lord should be :
And fulfilment crowned the promise given in sincerity.

EPODE.

From the dank depths rose an island, and the piercing sunbeams' Sire 70
Rules therein in glory ever, lord of steeds whose breath is fire.
There in wedlock Rhodus bare him sons, in skill surpassed of none,
Seven,—sire of Lindus one
And Ialysus his eldest and Camirus, each a king,
For their father's realms they parted, ruling each a peopled shire :
Still their names about their cities cling.

STROPHE.

There Tlepolemus with welcome expiation closed his pain,
Founder of another Tiryns : as a god, in sacrifice
Reeks for him the victim train,
And the lists are set for contests. There Diagoras triumphed twice, 80
Four times o'er in famous Corinth friendly fortune blessed him still,
Once and yet again in Nemea, and on Athens' rocky hill.

ANTISTROPHE.

Him the bronze of Argos, him the works on Theban anvil wrought,
Him Arcadia's prizes, and Bocotia's ritual games have known,
And Pellene. Home he brought
From Aegina triumphs six, nor other record Megara's stone
Bears of him. O Zeus, that rulest Atabyrium's summit high,
Father, bless the tuneful pageant of Olympic victory !

EPODE.

Ever be our famous champion crowned with worship and with grace,·
Of his townsmen both and strangers, for his feet unswerving trace 90
    Paths averse from pride, with lore of noble parents learnt aright.
    Never may oblivion's night
    Shroud the line of Callianax! For now the state holds festival,
With the Eratids rejoicing : yet full oft in shortest space
    Veers with sudden sweep the fickle gale !

OLYMP. VIII.

TO ALCIMEDON OF AEGINA, VICTOR IN THE BOYS'
WRESTLING MATCH.

STROPHE.

OLYMPIA, mother of the gold-crowned feasts,

Queen of true oracles ! where noble priests

In the blazing altars find Signs to read the Thunderer's mind,

And learn if any word hath Zeus to send

For souls, with desire

That to glory aspire,

Thus in peace their toils to end.

ANTISTROPHE.

So blest is piety, and fulfilled its prayer !

But thou, O Pisan grove of olives fair,

Bid our wreathèd revel band Welcome to Alpheüs' strand ;   10

For great his glory, who hath won thy meed !

To each in his measure

Heaven gives of its treasure ;

Many paths to blessings lead.

D

EPODE.

Sons of a house, from Zeus that springs ! His will,
   Timosthenes, gave Nemea's prize to thee :
And to Alcimedon, by Cronus' hill,
   Olympian victory.
Wrestler of fairest form and deeds as fair,
Aegina's seamen-sons his triumphs share :   20
   Where Justice sits in honour due,
    Throned by Zeus to strangers true.

STROPHE.

So o'er no folk she reigns! Of issues great
The complex poise aright to estimate,
Hard it is : but Heaven's command Draws the sons of every land
   Around this isle, set in the girdling main
    As a pillar sublime,
    And ever may Time
   Tireless still such task sustain !

ANTISTROPHE.

From Aeacus down, that land have Dorians swayed :—   30
Aeacus, whom great Poseidon erst to aid
Did with Leto's offspring call, High to rear Troy's rising wall,
   Foredoomed of Fate, from its embattled tower,
    (When war's fell affrays
    Should in havock outblaze,)
   Ruin's lurid fumes to pour.

EPODE.

Up-leaped upon the city's new-built wall
    Three sheeny snakes. Two, back in ruin thrown,
Crashed suddenly, and perished in their fall :
    One rushed exulting on !   40
Straight of the portent Phoebus spake his thought,
" Hero, Troy falls !—breached, where thy hands have wrought.
    " ' Tis thus I read this mystic sign
    " Sent of Thunder's lord divine.

STROPHE.

" Troy to thy sons of first and fourth descent
" Shall bow !" He spake, and straight careering went
Forth to Xanthus, and the meads Scoured of Amazonian steeds,
    And Ister : while in charioted flight
        The Trident-armed king
        To the Isthmus did bring   50
Aeacus on steeds of light.

ANTISTROPHE.

And there he ruled steep Corinth's festival.—
But, (since, Melesias ! nought seems sweet to all,)
Though thy praise, that now I sing, But from boyish victories spring
    Yet may I scape the stroke of Envy's stone.
        For in Nemea eke,
        With these, will I speak
Triumphs of thy pupils won

EPODE.

'Mid men in the Pancratium! Who would train,
　　Must first himself have learned, or pass for fool.　　60
Sage inexperience boasts its craft in vain.
　　And who so well should school
Aspiring youth, in every path that leads
To lovely fame and hallowed victory's meeds,
　　As thou, for whom Alcimedon
　　Thirtieth triumph now hath won?

STROPHE.

Matching, with all that man may do, Heaven's grace,—
Four rivals met,—he spurned the craven's case,
Home that slinks with dull retreat, Shamefast tongue, and stealthy
　　　　feet.
　　His aged grandsire thrilled with quickening joy,　　70
　　　　And eld was forgot—
　　　　Such prosperous lot
　　Death's blind terrors can destroy.

ANTISTROPHE.

But I must wake remembrance, and unfold
The glories won by Blepsiad hands of old.
Six proud garlands now they claim, Won in many a leaf-crowned
　　　　game.

The very dead, through ritual meet, may share
    Such fame : nor the gloom
    Of the mouldering tomb
Hides their kinsman's triumph fair.   80

EPODE.

Iphion, (by Rumour, Hermes' daughter, taught,)
    Shall to Callimachus repeat, what pride
Zeus in Olympia to their house hath brought.
    With blessings multiplied
Still may He crown its sons ; nor sickness blight,
Nor angered Nemesis their glories spite !
    No, still may He, with flawless fate,
    Make their clan and city great !

OLYMP. IX.

TO EPHARMOSTUS OF OPUS, VICTOR IN WRESTLING.

STROPHE.

ARCHILOCHUS' three-fold lay,
In Olympia sounded forth, the swelling triumph-song,
    Served by Cronus' hill to guide the way
Of Epharmostus and his comrade-throng.
    But now a shaft of stronger flight befits
    The Muses' bow. Be Zeus our aim, that sits
        'Mid glare of lightnings bright
        On Elis' honoured height,
Hippodamia's glorious dowry, won
Of old by Pelops, Lydia's hero-son.   10

ANTISTROPHE.

And speed me an arrow sweet,
Pytho-wards, of wingèd song, that soars and spurns the ground !
    Strike the harp our wrestler bold to greet,
And be proud Opus and her son renowned !
    Opus, that Justice with her daughter sways—
    Eunomia, guardian queen,—and blooms in praise,

By Castaly, and o'er
Alpheüs' stream-washed shore,
The glorious land, whence proudest chaplets come,
The mother of fair trees, the Locrians' home.   20

EPODE.

His city dear will I adorn
    With fiery songs of loudest strain.
Swifter than noblest courser borne,
    Or sail-fledged ships that cleave the main :
Afar will I the tale recite.
    If, Graces sweet, 'tis mine in humblest share
    To cull the blossoms of your garden rare—
For yours is all that charms : and Heaven sends skill and might.

STROPHE.

Ne'er save by such aid upheld
Heracles with brandished club had met the trident's blow :   30
    When Poseidon his assault repelled
From Pylos, and Apollo bent the bow,
    Nor Hades spared that fatal rod to shake,
    Guided whereof the dead their journey take
        The vaulted path along—
        Nay, quit such theme of song,
Tongue mine ! The craft that dares with impious taunts
Assail the Gods, I loathe : and misplaced vaunts

ANTISTROPHE.

Are songs for a madman's string !

Prate not thus : but from the Gods sweep far the tale of fight, 40

And Protogeneia's city sing—

Where led of Zeus, that hurls the lightnings bright,

Down from Parnassian heights Deucalion came

With Pyrrha Man's primeval home to frame,

And there, sans travail, won

Descendants sprung from stone,

Laians * thence named.   Let these inspire your voice ;

And of old wine, but new-blown song make choice !

EPODE.

For earth, 'tis told in story, sank

Whelmed 'neath a dark and raging main,   50

But sudden, cleft of Zeus, she drank—

The swollen surge was pent again !

The shielded warriors, whence springs

Your house, were of these children of the rock :

Their mothers dames of Iapetian stock,

Zeus-born their sires : and still the country owns them kings.

STROPHE.

Not yet had the Thund'rer riven

Opus' child from her Epeian home, his love to be

---

* Greek, Λᾶας = "a stone."

On Maenalian heights,—and, after, given
To Locrus, lest unblest of progeny   60
   His days should close. Ere long a Zeus-sprung boy
   She bare, whose beauty thrilled her lord with joy ;
      And Opus bade him share
      The name himself did bear ;
   Then to the wondrous youth, so fair and brave,
   A city and a nation's care he gave.

ANTISTROPHE.

And round him a stranger host
Flocked from Arcady and Pisa, Thebes and Argos, sent.
   But Aegina's son and Actor's most
He loved,—Menaetius ; sire of him that went   70
   With Atreus' sons to Troy, sole faithful found
   To wronged Achilles, when the fleet around
      'Mid rout of valiant Greeks
      Raged Telephus. Still speaks
   His fame, and wise men know Patroclus' might !
   Thenceforth, amid the crash of furious fight

EPODE.

The son of Thetis bade him stand
   The nearest ever to his side,
Sheltered of his victorious brand.—
   Fain would I still in fancy ride   80

On Muses' chariot meetly borne,

    With daring vigour filled, and passion's flame :

    But Worth, Lampromachus, and Friendship claim

My praise for Isthmian wreaths, that thee and Him adorn—

STROPHE.

    Thy kinsman. In one proud day

Triumphed each, and twice ye knew, in Corinth, contest's joy.

    Victories were his by Nemea's bay,

And Argos crowned the man,—Athens the boy !

      But, oh, when now to manhood newly grown

      He sought the silver prize in Marathon,   90

          And there with footing true

          And rapid feint o'erthrew

      Each senior tried, what shouts rang round to greet

      The fair young hero of so fair a feat !

ANTISTROPHE.

    His might the Parrhasians saw

When at Zeus' Lycaean games he dared their wondering hosts.

    Home he brought that charm for winter's flaw,

Pellene's cloak. Of him Eleusis' coasts,

      And Iolaus' grave, in witness speak.

      'Tis native might speeds best :—there are, that seek   100

          By tutored worth to aim

          Presumptuously at fame.

But mortal schemes of Providence unblest
As well in mute oblivion may rest.

EPODE.

All paths may not alike avail,
Not one pursuit may all men raise,
For skill's ascent is hard to scale.
Yet lives there one may claim such praise,
Then loud and bold his fame resound :—
The victor, graced with blessings from on high,   110
Strong arm, lithe limb, and spirit-speaking eye,
Whose hand at Ajax' feast the Ilian altar crowned.

OLYMP. X.

*TO AGESIDAMUS OF WESTERN LOCRIS IN SICILY, VICTOR IN
THE BOYS' WRESTLING MATCH. A PRELIMINARY ODE
PROMISING ANOTHER TO FOLLOW.*

STROPHE.

TIMES there are, when winds best serve our need,
    Or waters from the sky,
    The rain-cloud's progeny ;
But honeyed song, when dauntless toils succeed,
    Still to fresh praise gives birth,
    And stamps its warrant on exalted worth.

ANTISTROPHE.

Who from Pisa's victor would withhold
    This monument of fame?
    Such theme my tongue shall claim,
If Heaven empower this mortal to unfold   10
    Poesy's bright flowers : and so,
    Agesidamus, for thy prowess know—

EPODE.

Son of Archestratus—my songs ancw
    Shall gild your golden bays,
    And bring the clans of Western Locrians praise.
Haste hither, Muses, join our revel crew!
For, trust me, here no folk shall meet your view,
    Harsh to strangers, blind to culture's charms,
    Nay, but in wisdom peerless, and in arms!
And when did tawny foxes yet,   20
Or lions fierce, their instinct's laws forget?

OLYMP. XI.

*ON THE SAME VICTORY AS THE PRECEDING; A FULFIL-
MENT OF THE PROMISE THERE MADE, WITH APOLOGIES
FOR ITS LATENESS.*

STROPHE.

OF Archestratus' son, That at Pisa won,
 The name deep-graved in my soul recite !
A lay I vowed him, and lo ! my vow Lies all forgotten. Yet, Muse,
    do thou,
  And Truth, Zeus' daughter, with hand of might
   From such reproach the bard defend,
   As paints him false to a trusting friend !

ANTISTROPHE.

For though length of delay, Since that far-back day,
 Hath turned to shame me the debt I owe,
The boon may Usury yet increase, And bid the carpings of slander
    cease.
  Say, whither then down the torrent's flow   10
   Our swift stone speed we ? how aright,
   Our debt discharging, our friend delight ?

EPODE.

For Truth the Western Locrian's city sways :
Homage to Song's fair queen it pays,
And Ares mailed : and there in fight Bold Cycnus stemmed Alcides'
    might.
    But for his triumph in Olympia's ring
    Let Agesidamus bring
        To Ilas thanks, for so
            Patroclus erst repaid
        Achilles : hearts, with inborn worth that glow,   20
May Instruction spur to proudest heights of fame with heavenly aid.

STROPHE.

To success without pain May but few attain,
    That past all triumphs doth life illume.
But Heaven's just mandates my lays impel, Of mighty Heracles'
    sports to tell,
    That erst he founded by Pelops' tomb,
        What time,—His son, that rules the main,—
        The haughty Cteatus he had slain,

ANTISTROPHE.

Ay, and Eurytus too ! When his labour's due
    Perforce from Augeas fierce he took,

Beneath Cleonae concealed he lay, And smote them down on their

reckless way ;   30

For, couched in secret Eleian nook,

Routed had they in days gone by

His own Tirynthian chivalry,

EPODE.

Those proud Moliones ! And the king ere long,

That dared to do the stranger wrong,

Beheld his home with riches stored Laid waste by vengeful flame and

sword ;

While fast in deepest gulfs of ruin down

Sank his loved Epeian town.

A stronger foe to cast

Aside we strive in vain,   40

So he in headstrong folly lingering last

Faced the sacking of his city, nor from Death escape might gain.

STROPHE.

Then his warriors all Did the hero call

At once to Pisa the spoil to bring,

And Zeus' strong son for his Sire did found A temple of trees, and

fenced around

An open plot for his meted ring

And to glad revel gave the plain

Around,—such reverence pleased to deign

ANTISTROPHE.

With the Twelve Gods supreme To Alpheüs' stream,—
    And named from Cronus the snow-sprent heights,   50
The hill Oenomaus erst had swayed—*Then* nameless.   Nor failed the
        Fates to aid
    With welcome presence the natal rites !
        But aye on Time's unerring test
        Truth's self for credence alone must rest,

EPODE.

And Time sped onward bringing all to light.
    For lo ! with sacrificial rite
Calling each God the spoils to share, Quinquennial feast he founded
        there,
    While victors on that first Olympic day
    Bore its earliest meeds away.
        To whom did Fate allot   60
        The newly offered crown ?
        Strong arm, sure foot, and rapid chariot,——
Who were they whose prowess won them in the glorious strife
        renown ?

STROPHE.

In the stadium best, To the goal that pressed,
    Thy son, Licymnius ! shewed his speed,
Oeonus, leader of Midea's host : Tegea of Echemus made her boast
    In wrestling famed : and the boxers' meed

E

To Tiryns town Doryclus bore:
Mantinean Samus with coursers four

ANTISTROPHE.

In the chariots won—Halirothius' son: 70
    And all unerring flew Phrastor's spear:
With strength unrivalled Eniceus flung The massy stone in his grasp
            that swung,
    And loud and long was his comrades' cheer!
        Then o'er the lists with welcome ray
        The fair moon glittered, and closed the day.

EPODE.

And straight around rang from each banquet sweet
Such songs as yet the victors greet.
True to the primal rites we'll raise The strain, in these our later days,
    From victory named; and chant the bolt of fire,
    Launched of Zeus the mighty Sire,   80
        That speaks in thunder's crash,
            And greeteth triumph aye
        With lightning's vivid flash;
While full voices raise responsive to the vocal reed their lay,

STROPHE.

That by Dirce revered In its time appeared!
    Oh, passing dear is the late-born son,

When youth lies far from the aged sire : And love and rapture his
    bosom fire,
  For thoughts of wealth to a stranger gone,
   That alien masters now must sway,
   Do most embitter life's closing day !   90

ANTISTROPHE.

 So should champions brave To the silent grave,
  Agesidamus, unsung descend :
'Twere brief joy purchased with empty pain. But lo ! to thee doth
    the lyre's sweet strain,
  And tuneful flutings new lustre lend :
   The while Zeus' daughters far and wide,
   Maids of Pieria, spread thy pride !

EPODE..

 With eager joy the glorious house I greet.
 Watering with dews of honey sweet
The Locrians' well-peopled state, Thy noble son I celebrate,
 Archestratus,—as erst I saw him gain   100
 Victory by Olympia's fane
  On that auspicious day,
   In form and feature fair,
  Blent with such youthful bloom, as drove decay
Far from Ganymede, and brought him heavenly life with Zeus to
  share.

OLYMP. XII.

TO ERGOTELES OF HIMERA, VICTOR IN THE LONG FOOT-RACE.

STROPHE.

CHILD of Zeus, the Liberator, hear !
Be to Himera—Protectress !—near,
    Fortune ! For the barks that scour the sea,
    And wild wars on land are ruled of thee,
And wise debates : but ever, high or low,
Man's hopes toss on, and stem Delusion's shifting flow.

ANTISTROPHE.

Never yet to mortal man, from Heaven,
Presage sure of things to be was given.
    Blind the skill that would the future scan !
    Many a hap, undreamed of, falls to man,   10
Wrecking his joy ; while some engulfed in pain
Find soon their sorrows turned to depth of bliss again.

EPODE.

Son of Philanor ! 'mid thy countrymen,
Cooped like a cock from foes beyond the pen,
 Thy speed had shed its blooms, to fame unknown !
But faction rose ; thy home to thee was lost.
 Now at Olympia thou hast donned the crown,
And twice at Pytho, and by Corinth's coast ;
 Pride of the Nymphs' Warm Springs ; with new lands of thine own !

OLYMP. XIII.

TO XENOPHON OF CORINTH, ON HIS DOUBLE VICTORY IN THE FOOT-RACE AND THE PENTATHLON,—A COMBINA-TION OF FIVE DIFFERENT GAMES, AS QUOIT-THROWING, LEAPING, ETC.

STROPHE.

WHILE the house, at Pisa crowned
    With triumph thrice, its townsmen's boast,
To strangers kind, I praise : my lays shall sound
    The fame of Corinth's favoured coast,
        Isthmian Poseidon's porch, home of bright youth.
Eunomia, and her sisters twain, The state's foundations there sustain,
Justice, and Peace of kindred mind, Whose bounteous hands enrich
        mankind,
        Daughters divine of law-abiding Truth!

ANTISTROPHE.

Proud Presumption, rash of speech,
    Mother of Discord, these repeL   10
Fair is my theme : and vigour bold shall teach
    My ready tongue its praise to telL

'Tis hard to hide the stamp that birth imparts :
And, children of Aletes, ye May boast of many a victory,
Whose meed exalted Valour claims, Triumphant in the hallowed games,
And many a seed of wisdom in your hearts

EPODE.

By flowery Hours implanted erst.   Each art is theirs that found it first.
And who but ye the Bacchic feast did rear,
Bold Dithyrambs to guerdon with the steer?
Who meted first the armed equestrian race ?   20
With eagles twain who first did temples grace?
And yours are Music's sweetest strains,
And 'mid your youthful spearmen Ares reigns.

STROPHE.

Throned upon Olympian hill,
O sovereign Zeus, to this my lay
Grant, Father, thine ungrudging favour still !
This nation's weal protecting aye,
Waft on the prosperous fate of Xenophon—
And bless his wreathed revel train, That here he leads from Pisa's plain!
For he the five-fold contest's meed, And eke hath gained the prize of
speed,—   30
Such fame as never other mortal won.

ANTISTROPHE.

Twice his victor-brows were crowned,
    For prowess shown in Isthmian games,
With parsley twine. Nor Nemea on him frowned.
    And Thessalus his father claims
        Renown for speed beside Alpheüs' shore;
Diaulus, stadium,—each he won, At Pytho, 'neath a single sun;
And, ere a moon had waned, his locks—Where Athens soars on
        beetling rocks—
    The glories of a triple triumph wore!

EPODE.

Seven times her crown Hellotia gave, And from the lists by Corinth's
    wave,   40
    With Ptoeodore his sire, yet prouder fame,
    With Eritime and Terpsias, to him came.
And then in Delphi, and the Lion's brake,
His single prowess boldly will I stake
    'Gainst many a hero's feats combined,
    Vast as the sands, whose count I may not find!

STROPHE.

Now—for limit all obeys,
    And wise is he that knows its due!—
Must I, that in my freight of public praise
    Have ventured private glories too,   50

Tell, how in skill of old and prowess brave
Was Corinth famed : nor false my song, Of Sisyphus divinely strong
In craft ; and how Medea defied A father's wrath, and fled —a bride,
Ship Argo and its warrior-crew to save !

ANTISTROPHE.

And, in other days, their might
Before Troy's ramparts these displayed,
And strove on either side, and swayed the fight.
To Atreus' sons some lent their aid
Helen to win,—with equal valour some
Withheld her still, and Danaans feared, When Lycian Glaucus' form
appeared ; 60
Before them all with pride he told, " How ruled his sire Pirene's hold,
" With wealthy heritage, and lordly home."

EPODE.

Long toiled beside Pirene's spring That sire, while 'neath his yoke to
bring
The Gorgon's offspring, Pegasus, he sought.
Till Pallas pure the golden bridle brought.
From out his dreams she rose in vision clear,
And cried, " Aeolian king ! yet sleep'st thou here ?
" Lo ! take this charm to quell your steed,
" And be a snow-white bull The Tamer's meed !"

STROPHE.

Lapt in darkness as he slept,　　　　　　　　　　7(

  Such words the goddess seemed to say.

And seizing straight, as to his feet he leapt,

    The mystic gift that by him lay,

      He sought Coiranides, the nation's seer ;

And sped with eager joy to tell, " What issues wonderful befell,

" How at the altar as he lay, His prophet-mandate to obey,

    " The child of Zeus, that hurls the lightning's spear,

ANTISTROPHE.

" Brought the spirit-quelling gold ! "

  The prophet bade him swift obey,

And when to Him, whose might doth Earth uphold,　　　8c

    The strong-limbed victim he should slay,

      Straight to the Equestrian Queen an altar found !

The power of Heaven can lightly deign Boons, that Hope's self despairs

    to gain :

And bold Bellerophon with speed Won to his will the wingèd steed

    Binding that soothing spell his jaws around.

EPODE.

Mounting, all mailed, his charger's pace The dance of war he taught

    to trace.

  And, borne of him, the Amazons he slew,

    Nor feared the bows their woman-armies drew,

Chimaera breathing fire, and Solymi,—
Sweeping from frozen depths of lifeless sky.
    Untold I leave his final fall !—
    His charger passed to Zeus' Olympian stall.

90

STROPHE.

But the whirling shafts I ply
    No longer from the mark must stray,
With devious aim : for hither pleased I hie,
    The fair-throned Muses to obey,
        And vindicate the Oligaethids' fame
In Nemea and Isthmus eke. Few words their many feats may speak :
For witness bears the tuneful cry Of herald sworn, that may not lie,
        To sixty triumphs thence that to them came.

100

ANTISTROPHE.

Well, ere now, my song hath told
    Of their Olympic victories ;
And what shall be, must coming lays unfold.
    Yet hope have I,—the future lies
        With Fate,—yet bless but Heaven still their line,
Ares and Zeus shall all fulfil ! For, by Parnassus' frowning hill,
Argos, and Thebes, their fame how fair ! And, oh, what witness soon
        shall bear,
        In Arcady, Lycaeus' royal shrine

EPODE.

Pellene, Sicyon, of them tell,—Megara, and the hallowed dell
   Of Aeacids; Eleusis; Marathon bright;   110
   And wealthy towns that bask 'neath Aetna's height;
Euboea's island. Nay, all Greece explore,—
Than eye can see, you'll find their glories more!
   Through life, great Zeus, sustain their feet;
   And bless with piety, and with triumphs sweet!

OLYMP. XIV.

TO ASOPICHUS OF ORCHOMENUS, VICTOR IN THE BOYS'
FOOT-RACE.

STROPHE.

GRACES, that your homes have placed
Where Cephisus' stream enriches lands with noble coursers graced !
Queens of melody, that hold
Bright Orchomenus, protectors of the Minyan nation old !
List, while to you I make my prayer : For all things sweet, and all
       things fair,
Are showered of you on mortals' state,
To make them wise, or fair, or great !
    Nay, never dance nor banquet yet
The Gods ordained, but ye were nigh. For all the pleasures of the sky
    Your hands dispense ; and high your thrones are set   10
By Pythian Phoebus with his bow of gold,
There in never-ending honour the Olympian Sire ye hold !

ANTISTROPHE.

Great Aglaia, hear my lay !
Sweet Euphrosyne ! Ye daughters of the God of strongest sway !

Hear, Thalia, queen of song !

Watch with favouring gaze as lightly trips our joyous revel-throng

Tis young Asopichus I sing, And Lydian measures with me bring,

And Lydian lays,—the Minyan name

Owes to thy grace Olympic fame.

Haste, Echo, to the gloomy cell,　　　　　　　　　20

Where reigns Persephonè : and there, To greet his sire, the tidings bear.

And of his son's renown Cleudamus tell :

How, by the glens of glorious Pisa, he

Crowned his young locks with plumes of victory !

PYTHIAN I.

TO HIERO, VICTOR IN THE CHARIOT-RACE, FOUNDER OF THE NEW CITY AETNA, WHICH HE COMPLIMENTED BY ASSOCIATING ITS NAME WITH HIS OWN IN THE PRO-CLAMATION OF HIS VICTORY.

STROPHE.

GOLDEN lyre, that Phoebus shares with the Muses violet-crowned !
    Thee, when opes the joyous revel, our frolic feet obey.
And minstrels wait upon the sound,
    While thy chords ring out their preludes, and guide the dancers' way.
Thou quenchest the bolted lightning's heat,
And the eagle of Zeus on the sceptre sleeps, and closes his pinions fleet.

ANTISTROPHE.

King of birds ! His hookèd head hath a darkling cloud o'ercast,
    Sealing soft his eyes. In slumber his rippling back he heaves,
By thy sweet music fettered fast.
    Ruthless Ares' self the muster of bristling lances leaves,   10
And gladdens awhile his soul with rest.
For the shafts of the Muses and Leto's son can melt an Immortal's
    breast.

EPODE.

But whom Zeus loves not, back in fear All senseless cower, as in
    their ear
The sweet Pierian voices sound, In earth or monstrous Ocean's round.
    So he, Heaven's foe, that in Tartarus lies,
The hundred-headed Typho, erst
In famed Cilician cavern nurst,—
Now, beyond Cumae, pent below
    Sea-cliffs of Sicily, o'er his rough breast rise
Aetna's pillars, skyward soaring, nurse of year-long snow !   20

STROPHE.

Gushing thence with purest flow from the secret cavern stream
    Deadly fires. By day in torrents of lurid smoke they sweep ;
But nightly forth, with blood-red gleam,
    Curling flames hurl rocks in thunder adown the level deep.
And fiercest the fire-jets upward sent
By the monster engaolèd, the gazer's dread, the listener's wonderment !

ANTISTROPHE.

Bound he lies 'neath Aetna's floor, 'neath its summits dark with trees ;
    Stones for coverlet scar all his back as he cowers o'erthrown.
Oh, grant, great Zeus, I thee may please,
    In that rich land's brow that reignest !—whose namesake neigh-
    bour town.   30

A founder renowned hath glorified,

For, when Hiero triumphed on Pytho's course, *her* titles the herald cried !

EPODE.

The vessel's course with joy begins, A favourable breeze that wins—

E'en as she quits the land—to bear The shipmen whither they would fare :

    For so on as glad return they count.

And in this first success we see

Equestrian triumphs yet to be,

And joyous feasts, where song shall sound.

    O Lord of Delos, and Castalia's fount,

Lycian Phoebus ! grant our prayer, and bless this land with sons

    renowned ! 40

STROPHE.

Gods alone the gifts can grant, that to mortals glory bring.

    Wisdom comes of them, and valorous arm, and skilful tongue,

Yet, though a mortal's praise I sing,

    Hope have I, my dart—not idly beyond the barriers flung—

Afar shall surpass each rival's throw.

Ay, still be his future with blessings fraught, and to memory lost his woe.

ANTISTROPHE.

Still shall coming years recall, how with steadfast heart he bore

    Brunt of war's affrays, and Heaven to his house accorded fame.

F

Never gathered Greek before
    Crown of wealth so fair! As erst Philoctetes, forth he came   50
To battle. (The proudest lord at need
Must stoop for alliance to sue. And so, for the archer of Poeas' seed

EPODE.

Came the great heroes, stories say, In Lemnos wounded as he lay,
And Priam's town of him was ta'en, And ended all the Danaans' pain.
    Though halting his step, Fate's will was done!
And thus may Heaven's restoring powers
Grant Hiero's will in coming hours!)
The tidings of this triumph bring,
    Muse, to Deinomenes. Full well may son
Share a father's joy: then raise we songs of praise to Aetna's king!   60

STROPHE.

His the state that Hiero founded in liberty divine,
    True to Hyllic type abiding: (Pamphylians ever thus,
And children of Heraclid line,
    Cleave to laws Aegimian, dwelling beneath Taÿgetus.
From Pindus their favoured fathers came
To Amyclae, and there by the Tyndarid's shrine they flourished in
      martial fame.)

ANTISTROPHE.

Blessings evermore by Amenas' wave, great Zeus, accord
    Thus to prince and people, thus be their praise not sung in vain !
From sire to son, each nation's lord
    Learns of Thee alone, in love o'er a loyal state to reign.   70
Oh, grant that in peace the mingled host,
Phoenician and Tuscan, henceforth may dwell, late vanquished on
        Cumae's coast !

EPODE.

Mourn they at home their navies brought, By Syracusa's king to nought,
Who, headlong from the swift ship's side, Their warriors hurled beneath
        the tide,
    And rescued Hellas from serfdom sore.
For Salamis be Athens famed ;
Nor less brave Sparta's feats proclaimed,
That laid beneath Cithaeron low
    The archer-Medians ! But, by Himera's shore,
Guerdon we with praise the might of Hiero's house, that crushed the
        foe !   80

STROPHE.

Seasoned praise, together gathering all in shortest scope,
    Best may shun reproach : for ever excess with chilling cloy
Weighs down the eager step of Hope,

But in townsmen's breasts broods deepest the grudge at alien joy.
Still—better be envied than pitied !—let
Fair fame never slip, steer thy people aright, and thy tongue on Truth's
       anvil whet !

ANTISTROPHE.

Lightest word thy lips escaping seems fraught with issues vast !
    Many claim thy care, and witness of thee for good or ill.
Then still to blooming worth cling fast,
    Grudge not for thy lavish gifts, if our praises charm thee still ! 90
But, mariner-like, spread free the sail;
Nor, by cunning deluded, forget that fame lives ever, though life may
       fail.

EPODE.

Men pass away, yet fame survives, To point the moral of their lives.
They last in tale or song enshrined.   Nor fades the praise of Croesus
       kind !
    But Phalaris dire, with his bull of brass,
The toils of infamy surround :
Nor lyres, in vaulted halls that sound,
To youths' glad songs admit his name !
    First among blessings Joy, next Praise I class ;
But, at both who aims, and wins them, proudest triumph-crown may
       claim !   100

PYTHIAN II.

TO THE SAME HIERO, VICTOR IN THE CHARIOT-RACE.

(*This is not really a Pythian Ode, for the success it describes was won at Thebes.*)

STROPHE.

HOME of War's fierce God, O Syracuse, city fair!

Land where warriors brave and martial steeds are bred!

Lo, to you am I come, from beauteous Thebes to bear

Triumph-songs, that tell how the earth-shaking car hath sped.

For borne thereon hath Hiero gained

Resplendent wreaths, Ortygia's brows to shade,

The river-home of Artemis, whose aid

Taught his pliant hands to tame the coursers deftly reined.

ANTISTROPHE.

She, the archers' queen, and Hermes that rules the race,

Deck with either hand his trappings; what time he yokes   10

Gallant steeds to the polished car with its guiding trace,

And the mighty God of the Trident with prayer invokes.

For other kings have bards of old,

Guerdoning worth, bade tuneful music swell!

Oft thus of Cinyras the Cyprians tell,

Aphrodite's priest, beloved of Phoebus tressed with gold.

EPODE.

These, led of gratitude aright, With service meet good deeds requite:
  And so, Deinomenes' son, of thee
Sings at her door each Locrian maid, And looks abroad, no more
        afraid,
    From horrors of war by thy power set free!   20
        But Heaven's will bound Ixion, (stories say,)
            Whirled round on his wheel,
            This law to reveal,
        That still should gratitude good deeds repay.

STROPHE.

Sure that law he found! For him had the Gods above
  Welcomed to their joys, but ill might he bear his bliss:
Hera's self—the glad bride of Zeus—with his frenzied love
  Insolent he wooed, rushing madly on Guilt's abyss.
      Justly he suffered for his sin
      A signal doom! And all his woes were brought   30
      By two mad crimes :—one, that his pattern taught
        Mortals first with guilty craft to shed the blood of kin,—

ANTISTROPHE.

One, that in the secret cells of the palace vast
    Jove's own spouse he tempted! (Happy who knows his place!)
Into measureless shame Delusion the lover cast:
    Fooled, yet unresisting, he welcomed a Cloud's embrace,

Whose phantom charms the wittol lured,
In form of Heaven's proud Queen, fatally fair,
Shaped by Zeus' craft the sinner to ensnare !
    Thus his own dread doom of fourfold fetters he ensured ; 40

EPODE.

In everlasting chains confined, He speaks Heaven's message to
        mankind !
And offspring weird of the phantom came :—
Monster of unexampled birth, Unhonoured or in heaven or earth,
    She reared ; and Centaurus she named his name.
        To him Magnetian mares at Pelion's foot
           Strange progeny bare,
           Commingled that share
      The form of sire and dam, half man, half brute !

STROPHE.

Fate Divine alone crowns hopes with a happy end,—
    Fate, than eagle winged, or dolphin that cleaves the brine, 5
Swifter far. At her touch the haughtiest soul must bend ;
    Fadeless fame to others must all at her will resign.
      But quit we biting censure's strain !
Far off I marked, how ill the slanderer's plight,
Archilochus, that battened on his spite :—
    Wealth and wisdom meetly blent were choicer boon to gain !

ANTISTROPHE.

Wealth is thine, and bounty more may its powers unfold :
    Sovereign thou of mighty nation, and tower-crowned town!
Boasteth any, that ever Hellas in days of old
    Bare a son as peerless in wealth, or in high renown ?   60
      —Empty his vaunt, his labour lost !
    I'll climb Song's flowery prow, and there recite
    Thy valour's praise. Ever doth martial might
      Youthful vigour glorify. The prouder, then, thy boast :

EPODE.

For not thy worth in wars alone, Afoot or mounted, thou hast
      shown !
    But riper Wisdom's renown is thine,
Then fearless flows my praise and free. Farewell! these songs I
      send to thee,
    Like Tyrian wares o'er the foaming brine :
      Tuned to Aeolic string, Castorean lays !
        Then graciously greet   70
        Our minstrelsy sweet.
    Learn thy true self, and live it ! Children's praise

STROPHE.

Greets the fawning ape ! But well Rhadamanthus fares ;
    Wisdom's fruit that culled, nor inly in falsehood joys,
(—Whispered flattery's bait, that mortals too oft ensnares :—)
    Dupe alike and victim fell slanderers' guile destroys !

Theirs is the crafty fox's mood ;
Yet what, the while, such gainful cunning's gain?
Like loaded nets they drudge beneath the main,—
    I, the buoyant cork, that rides unscathed above the flood ! 80

ANTISTROPHE.

Slander's guileful speech falls powerless on Virtue's ear ;
    Fawning yet around, their cunning the traitors ply.
Ne'er such folly be mine ! Who loves me, I'll hold for dear
    Still ; and, wolf-like, still as a foe on my foemen fly,
        And doubling dart, now here, now there.
In every state the true man prospers most ;
Rules monarch there, or fierce plebeian host,
    Elders wise,—whate'er they be, that make its weal their care !

EPODE.

Why chide at Heaven, that now bestows Fair fame on these, and
        now on those?
Yet, yet the envious heart is pained. 90
Still grasping, straining still, at last It plants in its own bosom fast
    The anguishing wound, ere its quest be gained !
        Who lightly bows him to the yoke, does well :
            To kick at the goad
            But lengthens the road :—
        Mine be it, with welcome, 'mid the great to dwell !

PYTHIAN III.

*TO THE SAME HIERO, ON TWO VICTORIES IN THE
HORSE-RACE.*

STROPHE.

WOULD that to Philyra's son once more,

Old Chiron, (if my voice this universal prayer may swell,)

Might Fate the vanished life restore :

And Cronos' potent stock again bear rule in Pelion's dell,

The Centaur of the wilds ! that erst In love to men Asclepius nursed

Artificer of restful health, whose aid

Each various form of sickness stayed !

ANTISTROPHE.

Or e'er Ilithyia's grace

Brought him to birth, his mother, with Diana's golden darts,

(Child of chivalrous Phlegyas,)   10

Slain in her chamber, sank to halls of Death, by Phoebus' arts.

The wrath that never burns in vain, Wrath of Zeus' seed she dared disdain,

Deceive her sire, and alien suit approve :

Yet her had Phoebus deigned to love !

EPODE.

Fraught with his seed, the bridal board
　　She yet refused,—the nuptial song,
Wherewith full oft in sweet accord
　　At eventide the maiden-throng
Their new-wed playmate soothe ! Far, far away
　　Her passion wandered,—sad, yet frequent case ! 20
Of all mankind the most unwise are they,
Who, spurning all at hand that lies, To distant visions turn their eyes,
　　Trust to vain hopes, and fleeting phantoms chase !

STROPHE.

So guilty passion brought to shame
Fair-robed Coronis, welcoming a stranger's rash embrace,
　　From distant Arcady that came :
Yet 'scaped she not Apollo ! He in Pytho's holy place
Knew all, by surest witness taught, His own wise soul's unerring
　　　　thought.
　　Him falsehood mocks not ; God from him, nor Man
　　Hides aught of all they do or plan ! 30

ANTISTROPHE.

He marked her treacherous paramour,
Ischys the Eilatid ; and straight to Lacereia bade haste
　　His sister with resistless power,
For there by Boebias' rocky marge the maiden's home was placed

Thus Fate estrangèd laid her low With dire reverse, while in her woe
    Full many a neighbour shared, and with her fell:
    Thus one quick spark fires all the dell!

EPODE.

As on the pyre her kinsmen laid
    The damsel, ringed with lambent ray
Of eager flames, Apollo said,   40
    " I'll brook no more my son to slay,
"Whelmed in the mother's piteous fate!" He spake:
    Then from the corse, that at a bound he gains,
Draws forth his child,—the flames around him break!
Thence to the Magnete Centaur brought, Apollo's child of him was
    taught
    To free mankind form sickness' various pains.

STROPHE.

To him for aid each sufferer came,
With inbred ulcers mated long, or torn with gleaming sword,
    Or hurtling stone: each wasted frame,
That heat had scorched, or winter chilled, he rescued and
    restored!   50
And now he chants the magic strain, And now with potions soothes
    the pain:

Or swathes the limbs in healing bands : or plies
The steel, and lo ! the sick men rise !

ANTISTROPHE.

But greed can wisdom's self enthrall.
Lured by the gold, whose treacherous gleam the tempter's hand
    revealed,
From Death's domain he dared recall
The captive dead : but Cronos' son smote Healer both and healed !
The burning levin, fraught with death, Tore from their breasts the
    struggling breath.
Let mortals seek, what fits a mortal's state ;
And know their nature, and their fate !   60

EPODE.

Immortal life then covet not :
    Scheme we, soul mine, but what we may !
Yet oh, if still within his grot
    Dwelt Chiron sage, and this my lay
Had spells to bind his soul, him had I won
    E'en now to send such healer to the good,
(Of Phoebus or his sire, some trueborn son !)
My bark should cleave the Ionian foam, And seek the hospitable home
    Of Aetna's chief, by Arethusa's flood :—

STROPHE,

The lord of Syracuse, that ne'er   70
Frowned on Worth's rise : to townsmen kind, to strangers noblest
    friend !
    Oh, might I to him voyage, and bear
Twin blessings, Golden Health, and Song, that lustre new should lend
To Pytho's crown, the late-won meed In Cirrha of his Victor-steed !
    Then, wafted o'er the deep, had I from far
    Beamed on him brighter than a star !

ANTISTROPHE.

    But now to thee my vows I'll pay,
Mother of Gods : whom oft with Pan the maidens at my door
    Revere, dread Queen, in nightly lay !
Hiero ! thou know'st—for known to thee is all tradition's lore—   80
How, for each blessing Gods bestow, They add a double share of woe :
    Fools may not brook its weight, but wise men find
    The threatening cloud is silver-lined.

EPODE.

    Fate's constant favours round thee cling ;
      For, ever, potent Fortune best
    Of mortals loves the warrior-king.
      Yet was not Peleus' self *all* blest,

Nor godlike Cadmus : though of men (they say)
    Happiest were these, for on the mountain wild,
And in seven-gated Thebes they heard the lay   90
Of Muses golden-frontleted, When one with fair Harmonia wed,
    And one with Thetis famed, sage Nereus' child.

STROPHE.

    And Gods with either shared the board,
And gifts they gained from Cronos' sons throned on their chairs
        of gold.
    By favour thus of Zeus restored
From troubles overpast, again their hearts rose high and bold !
But bitter woes in later day Swept half of Cadmus' bliss away ;
    Three daughters,—hapless all ! albeit great Jove
    Left heaven for fair Thyone's love.

ANTISTROPHE.

    He fell too,—Peleus' offspring sole,   100
Of Thetis born in Phthia,—fell, struck by the deathful dart :
    His pyre awoke the Danaans' dole !
Oh, may each mortal still, that guides in wisdom's ways his heart,
Enjoy the full of Heaven's good gift ! For fickle breezes soar, and
        shift ;
    And when Prosperity falls full and strong
    On mortal's path, it bides not long !

EPODE.

Lowly I'd live in lowly state:
　And great, in greatness :—far as power
Is mine, I'll bow me to my fate !
　Should Heaven rich bounty on me shower,　　　110
Hereafter trust I fair renown to find.
　Famed Nestor and Sarpedon many a strain
Of cunning fabric yet recalls to mind—
Themes of a wide world's praises ! long Lives Virtue shrined in glorious
　　　　　song,
　But few there are, such bliss may lightly gain.

PYTHIAN IV.

TO ARCESILAS, KING OF CYRENE, A GREEK COLONY IN
AFRICA, VICTOR IN THE CHARIOT-RACE.

STROPHE.

MUSE, be thy place beside a friend to-day,
That rules Cyrene, land of steeds ! Arcesilas the revel leads :
To Leto's sons and Pytho pour with him the votive lay !
Pytho, where by Zeus' eagles sate of old,
And there, (of Phoebus not unaided,) told
The prophet-maid, how Battus' reign Should rise o'er Libya's fruitful
        plain,
Where he far from his island home should found
Car-famed town on gleaming mound.

ANTISTROPHE.

Thus he the seventh from the tenth in line
Should fill, whate'er in earlier age Medea, fired with prophet-rage, 10
Aeëtes' daughter, Colchian queen, poured from her lips divine.
'Mid warrior Jason's crew, " Give ear ! " she cried
" O sprung from Gods, and earthly chiefs of pride.

G

" I tell you, from this wave-beat earth She that from Epaphus hath
      birth

  " A germ of future towns, to mortals dear,

  " In Zeus Ammon's home shall rear !

EPODE.

" For the finny dolphin they shall urge the flying steed,

" Guiding with rein for oar the chariot's stormy speed.

  " That augury shall Thera mother make

" Of cities great:—the symbol clod, That erst a mortal-seeming God,   20

  " (Where gush the fountains of Tritonis' lake,) .

" Gave to Euphemus as he leaped ashore,

" While Cronian Zeus approval spake amid the levin's roar.

STROPHE.

  " He met us, as the anchor's fang we cast, .

" Swift Argo's curb, adown her side. For from the distant Ocean's tide

  " O'er barren steppes her sea-worn hull had journeyed twelve days
      past,

  " Drawn from the deep at my injunction wise.

  " There roaming lone the .God appeared, in guise

" Assumed of some kind mortal man ; And, smiling welcome, straight
      began

  " Such gracious words as greet an entering guest,   30

  " To the generous banquet prest.

ANTISTROPHE.

" But home's sweet pretext brooked not of delay.

" *Eurypylus*, he cries, *in me Behold: His son, that rules the sea!*

" Then grasping, (for our haste he knew,) such sods as nearest lay,

" Proffered the friendly gift with eager hand.

" And forth, not disobedient, on the strand

" Our champion leaped ; and from the God With palm responsive took
the sod.

" But, well I wot, at eve the briny spray

" Swept it down the water-way.

EPODE.

" On the helpful serving-men I oft had vainly wrought,   40

" Duly to guard the gift—oblivion dulled their thought !

" *Here* lies the germ of Libya's spacious state

" Shed ere its time. Ah ! had it come To that divine Taenarian home

" Where dwells Euphemus hard by Hades' gate,

" Equestrian Poseidon's son, the king

" Whom Tityus' daughter bare of yore beside Cephisus' spring :—

STROPHE.

" For then his offspring in the fourth degree

" That spacious continent had gained, With aid of Danaan hosts,
constrained

" From Argos and Mycenae and proud Sparta's realm to flee !

" But to him now an alien bride shall bear   50
    " A destined race, that, blest by heavenly care,
" Shall reach this isle, and there obtain A son to rule its loamy plain,
    " To whom, arrived at Pytho's gold-stored cell,
    " Phoebus shall his fate foretell :

ANTISTROPHE.

" How he his hosts must lead in later days,
" Embarking, to the wealthy land Of Cronus' son on Nilus' strand."
    So ran Medea's rhythmic speech, and dumb in blank amaze
    Cowered the great chieftains as her rede they heard.
    Blest son of Polymnastus, *thee* that word
Foretold ! The Delphian maid of *thee* Spake in unprompted augury ! 60
    And thrice she bade thee Hail,—ordained by fate
    Monarch of Cyrene's state !

EPODE.

Thus, when aid from heaven thou sought'st to loose thy speech's string,
Spake she. And now, though late, in prime as of flowery spring,
    Eighth of that line blooms an Arcesilas,
Whom, with equestrian triumph crowned, Phoebus and Pytho have
            renowned.
    Ye Muses ! at my bidding sound his praise ;
And sing the golden fleece,—that journey's aim,
That won the Minyan mariners wreaths of celestial fame.

STROPHE.

What earliest impulse bade them plough the sea ? 70
What peril's stubborn bond constrained? For Pelias death had Heaven
    ordained,
    By force, or craft relentless, of the famed Aeölidae.
    Chill on his wise soul struck the ominous word,
    By wood-crowned Mother Earth's mid navel heard,
That bade him, with unslackening care Of the "One-sandalled Man"
    beware,
    What time should he seek from the mountain height
    Famed Iolcos' champaign bright,

ANTISTROPHE.

Stranger or townsman ! And he came in time :
A hero dread, twin spears he bore ; And twinfold guise of raiment wore,
    For aptly to his wondrous limbs clove garb of Magnete clime,   80
    Nor rains might pierce the pardskin round him spread,
    Nor his bright locks unshorn their blooms had shed,
But mantled round his shoulders broad ! Swift to the market-place he
    strode,
    And testing all his dauntless mettle stood
    'Mid the gathering multitude.

EPODE.

Then those crowds unknowing questioned of him near and far :
"Phoebus he is not? Nay ! nor He of the brazen car

" That Cypris loved ;—in Naxos died, they say,
"Iphimedea's giant brood, Otus and Ephialtes rude.
    "And Tityus fell, to those keen shafts a prey   90
" That Artemis' unvanquished quiver drove ;
" Teaching mankind, within their powers to curb ambitious love."

STROPHE.

Such speech from one to other passed around.
And lo ! with polished car, mule-traced, Headlong sped Pelias hot with
    haste :
    Then spied, and shuddering knew too well, what *Single sandal*
    bound
The youth's right foot. Yet, forced his fears to hide,
" And what the home thou vauntest, friend ?" he cried,
" Of earth-born dames what mother erst In hoary eld such offspring
    nursed ?
    "Tell me thy lineage, nor dare defile
    " Tale so proud with falsehood vile."   100

ANTISTROPHE.

Thereat in gentle tones he, fearless, said :
" Trained in old Chiron's school I come, Whose daughters in their
    cavern-home,
    " Philyra and Chariclo,—spotless maids !—my childhood bred.
    "Now, twice ten years fulfilled, nor tongue nor hand
    " Offending e'er, I seek my native land ;

" To win the realm, where ruled of old My sire, now passed to alien hold,

    " Unrighteously,—for there did Zeus ordain

    " Aeolus and his sons should reign.

EPODE.

" Well I wot, hath Pelias, led by jaundiced greed astray,

" Torn from my sire perforce the land of his ancient sway.   110

    " And me ; when light dawned on my opening eyes,

" My parents mourning made, for dread Of that fierce lord, and

        feigned me dead,

    " And so, mid funeral gloom, and women's cries,

" Swathed me in purple bands, and darkling bare

" At midnight from my home, to dwell 'neath Chiron's fostering care.

STROPHE.

    " Thus hear ye briefly gathered all my rede ;

" And show me now, good townsmen mine, The cradle of my knightly

        line,

    " For sure no alien land is this to Aeson's native seed !

    " Jason am I,—the Centaur gave my name."

He spake : and to his aged father came,   120

Nor came unknown,—to greet the boy, Those time-worn eyes plashed

        tears of joy,

    For glad at heart was he, his son to find

    Choicest bloom of human kind.

ANTISTROPHE.

And Aeson's brethren, as the story spread,
Came flocking. First did Pheres hie From Hypereia's fount hard-by :
 And, from Messene, Amython : and with Admetus sped
 Melanthus, swift their kinsman dear to greet.
 Whom with all kindly speech did Jason meet,
Nor aught withheld of friendship's rights, But in the full of all delights
 Culled, five long days and nights, from hour to hour,   130
 Hallowed revel's fadeless flower.

EPODE.

Then the sixth day came, and graver theme did then unfold,
While in their ready ears the hero his purpose told.
 Swift from their seats they leapt ; and forth did fare
To Pelias' hall, then rushing in Expectant stood. Forth at the din
 Amazed came he whom bright-haired Tyro bare ;
And thus, with words firm set on Wisdom's base,
In gentle accents Jason spake : " Child of Poseidon's race !

STROPHE.

" The thoughts of man are all too swift to praise
" In place of justice crafty gain, Lead though it may to after pain.   140
 " But thou and I must rule our moods, and weave us happy days.
 " I speak not to a fool ! One dam of old
 " Gave birth to Cretheus and Salmoneus bold ;

" And on yon golden sun gaze we, *Their* children in the third degree.

" Fate frowns, whene'er in kindred bosoms rise

" Passions hiding kinship's ties.

ANTISTROPHE.

" Ill were it we the brazen sword should wield,

" Or launch the dart, and rend in twain The lordship of our sires' domain.

" Keep thou the flocks and herds of tawny kine ! thine be each field

" Thou from my sire hast torn to swell thy state !   150

" I grudge not though thy wealth grow ne'er so great.

" But that imperial sceptre's sway, That throne, whereon in earlier day,

" Judging this folk, sate he of Cretheus' line,

" —Spare us strife, and own them mine !

EPODE.

" Yield them thou, and shun the woes that from them else must rise."

Gently he spake, and thus as gently the king replies,

" Such will I be ! But round me now doth cling

" The lot of eld, while youth's bright flower Swells in thy veins, and thine is power

" To soothe Hell's vengeance : Phrixus bids us bring

" His prisoned sprite back from Aeëtes' home,   160

" And win that Ram's rich fleece, that bore him safe o'er Ocean's foam.

STROPHE.

" 'Scaping his stepdame's shafts of impious hate.

" This heard I in a wondrous dream ; And questioned, by Castalia's
   stream,

"*Seek must I aught ?*" And Phoebus bade prepare such convoy
   straight.

"This quest do thou fulfil, and straight will I

"Relinquish to thee rule and royalty :

"Be Zeus, the father of us both, The mighty witness of my oath !"

The chiefs applauding heard, and went their way :

Jason now his part must play !

ANTISTROPHE.

Heralds he sent to noise the tale around   170

Of purposed voyage, and swiftly came Three Zeus-sprung chiefs of
   warrior fame,

Alcmena's seed and Leda's. Came Poseidon's children, crowned

With lofty crest, and flushed with conscious might,

From Pylos hasting, and from Taenarus' height,—

Euphemus, Periclymenus, Your glory touched its zenith thus !

Next, Phoebus-born, the Sire of Song appeared,

Orpheus, name to praise endeared !

EPODE.

Golden-sceptred Hermes' twins the matchless task to share,

Joying in youth, Echion, Eurytus,—each was there !

Swift came those dwellers round Pangaeus' base, 180
Sent freely forth with willing mind By Him, their sire, that rules the
    wind,
    Zetes and Calais, sons of Boreas ;
Whose shoulders glowed in ruffling plumes attired !
Heaven's Queen such burning zeal in each heroic heart inspired.

STROPHE.

Each felt ship Argo's spell, nor might endure
To chew eld's cud and lonely bide In safety at his mother's side.
    Nay, come Death's self, each with his peers must seek zeal'
        glorious cure !
    So to Iolcos came that flower of crews ;
    Whom Jason with approval high reviews,
Meantime, with lots and auguries, His craft prophetic Mopsus plies, 190
    And bids the host embark. The anchor now
    Hangs expectant at the prow ;—

ANTISTROPHE.

The leader mounts the stern : his hands upraise
A golden cup; to Zeus he cries, Launcher of thunders, lord of skies ;
    To each swift blast of wind and wave ; to nights ; and Ocean's
        ways ;
    Fair seasons ; and kind Fate to bring them home !
    Forth from the clouds responsive thunders come

With fate-fraught roar, and broken rays Of fiery lightning round him
  blaze.
Then joyful breathed again those peers divine,
Strengthened by the heavenly sign.   200

EPODE.

" Ply the oar," the prophet cried, and joyous hopes inspired,
Swift in their sturdy grasp the oarage sped on untired.
    With favouring gales the Axine's mouth they near ;
Then to the ruler of the main, Poseidon, raise a hallowed fane,
    Where ruddy droves of Thracian kine appear,
And, (newly piled,) a hollow altar-stone :
So them the Lord of navies heard in depths of peril thrown !

STROPHE.

    Succour they prayed from the resistless jaws
Of clashing rocks, the fatal Twin, That lived and moved, more swift
  than din
    Of serried storm-winds, yet to them that voyage brought final
      pause.   .   210
    So came the hero band to Phasis' banks
    And met in fight the dusky Colchian ranks
E'en at Aeëtes' side. And then The queen of swiftest shafts to men
    The mystic wryneck's spell did first reveal
    Bound on the relentless wheel.

ANTISTROPHE.

That bird of frenzied love the Cyprian dame
From far Olympus' summit brought, And Aeson's prudent son she
    taught
To wile away with witching chant Medea's filial shame,
And fire with thoughts of Greece her love-smit breast.
From her he learnt to fill her sire's behest: 220
With mingled oil and magic banes, That quell the force of cruel pains,
    She bathed his frame, and each to each gave troth
    Wedlock sweet should link them both.

EPODE.

Then his plough of adamant Aëtes midst them sets,
While from his bulls the flames burst panting in yellow jets,
    And, rending earth, their brazen hoofs rebound.
Yet these he yoked, with none to aid, And straight the shapely fur-
    rows made,
    And scored a fathom deep the loamy ground,
Then spake, "This work accomplished, let the king
" That rules yon bark win from me that immortal covering,   230

STROPHE.

" His be the fleece tasselled with gleaming gold."
He spake, and Jason laid aside His saffron vest, and, fortified
    With trust in heaven, his task began : nor feared the flames, made
    bold

By his weird hostess' hest. The plough he grasped,
Round the bulls' necks constraining fetters clasped,
Smote with fierce goad each massy frame, And to his hard task's
ending came.
In speechless pain, yet groaning as amazed,
On his might Aeëtes gazed.

ANTISTROPHE.

Then to the hero 'gan his comrades reach
Welcoming hands, with wreathèd bays They roofed his brow, and
spoke his praise. 240
And Helios' wondrous offspring them of the bright fleece did teach,
Where stretched by Phrixus' sacring knives it lay ;
And deemed a task was here their hands to stay.
For to it clung, beneath the brake, With greedy fangs a monstrous snake,
Huge, as some penteconter's giant keel
Shaped amid the crash of steel.

EPODE.

Closer now time draws, 'twere long the beaten road to tread,
Learnt have I shorter paths, and others have in them led.
The bright-eyed, spangled snake by guile slew he ;
Medea—Pelias soon to slay!—By her own aid he stole away ; 250
And reached the floods of Ocean and Red Sea :
And those that killed their lords, the Lemnian dames.
There, for the vesture's meed, they showed their prowess in the games,

STROPHE.

And won them wives. That day, that night was sown
In foreign soil the germ, with fate Instinct, of Libya's glittering state ;
    Euphemus' race, that, planted then, hath greater ever grown;
    Whose children from their homes on Sparta's shore
    Spread to that isle, Callista named of yore.
Thenceforth did Leto's son ordain, Your sway should bless the Libyan .
        plain
    With sovereignty from heaven : for ye have found   260
    Counsels fraught with wisdom sound,

ANTISTROPHE.

    The golden-throned Cyrene's state to guide !
Try now like Oedipus thy skill On riddles! When with keen-edged bill
    A woodman lops some mighty oak, and mars its leafy pride :
    E'en in decay it testifies its worth,
    Whether in flames it end on winter's hearth,
Or, matched with comrade pillars tall, It prop a lordly palace wall,
    Painfully doomed in alien homes to toil,
    Banished from its native soil !

EPODE.

Grace to thee, apt healer of thy times, doth Paean lend,   270
Duly with soothing touch each ulcerous wound to tend.
    For feebler hands a town may lightly shake ;
But hard indeed the task, once more Its tottering fabric to restore,

Save of its rulers Heaven the guidance take!
Such task to thee hath Fate's fair web assigned,
Then still for blest Cyrene's weal toil on with ready mind.

STROPHE.

Of all wise Homer's precepts, ponder thou
This with the rest, " Good harbinger Doth grace on each behest
  confer."
 And sure, on righteous errand sped, Song's self doth nobler grow!
 Cyrene knows Demophilus' heart-truth,   280
 Battus' proud palace knows it ; with the youth
A very boy, yet every thought With a hoar century's wisdom fraught
 He silences the noisy tongue of spite,
 Schooled to loathe ungoverned might.

ANTISTROPHE.

 Not his against the good in strife to rave,
Or aught obstruct of Fate's sure plan: He knows · Time stays not
  long for man,
 So waits on Opportunity, its follower, not its slave !
 Yet his that sharpest pang,—at once to know
 The good, and yet perforce that good forego ;
Forth from his home, his country driven, He struggles, Atlas-like, with
  heaven.   290
 —But to the Titans gave great Zeus release,
 Sails may shift when tempests cease !

EPODE.

Yet he prays, when to the dregs is drained his cup of ill,
Home to return once more, and oft by Apollo's rill
    Give all his soul to joy ;—there, mid the throng
Poetic of his townsmen, bear The carven lyre, their quiet share,
    And never more, or do, or suffer wrong !
Then would he tell, what streams of deathless sound,
In hospitable Thebes, for great Arcesilas he found !

PYTHIAN V.

*ON THE SAME VICTORY AS THE PRECEDING. A HYMN FOR
THE TRIUMPHAL PROCESSION TO APOLLO'S TEMPLE AT
CYRENE.*

STROPHE.

POWER is Wealth's of wide extent,
   When mortals from the hand of destiny
Receive her, with unspotted virtue blent,
     A loved ally !
  Thereto divine Arcesilas,
    In triumph mounting—who but he ?—
   Of glorious life each proud degree,
Yoked with sweet praise doth ever nearer come ;
  By golden-charioted Castor's grace,
That now with sunshine after storms makes bright his happy home. 10

ANTISTROPHE.

Wise men wear with prudence meet
   The sovereignty that Powers of heaven bestow ;
And great the bliss that rings thy righteous feet :
    —First, king art thou
  Supreme o'er many a mighty town.

For in that honoured title most

Standeth thy kinsmen's common boast,

(And well therewith thy wisdom's streams combine !)

And next, to fill thy bliss, decked with renown

From Pytho's course, and home arrived, this triumph train is thine, 20

EPODE.

Such revel Phoebus loves ! Then ne'er forget,

As sounds thy praise round sweet Cyrene's grove,

Before all else the helpful god to set,

And of all friends Carrhotus most to love.

Not he to cloke defeat hath brought

Excuse, the child of Afterthought,

To yon proud halls of Battid kings.

But, by Castalia's springs

A welcome guest, the chariot's crown Round thy triumphant locks

hath thrown.

STROPHE.

Nor thy harness did he mar   30

In twelve swift courses round the holy place :

For all unbroken hangs the mighty car.

Each plaited trace,

Wherewith he flew past Crisa's hill,

By hands of skilful workmen wrought

Safe to the sacred vale he brought ;

That now its halls of cypress them contain,

    Hard by the statue's base, by Cretan skill

Formed of a single tree, and reared in that Parnassian fane.

ANTISTROPHE.

Who hath done this service rare,   40

    Well mays't thou with thy readiest welcome greet !

O Alexibius' son, the Graces fair

        Thy praise repeat.

    O favoured soul, that lasting pride,

        Albeit through weary toil, hast won !

        With calm strong purpose pressing on,

Mid forty fallen guiders of the rein,

    Secure through all didst thou thy chariot guide;

And, from the games returned, hast reached thy home on Libya's

        plain.

EPODE.

None is, nor shall be, all exempt from woe :   50

    But still on Battus Fortune's varied store

Is shed,—his city's tower, a light whose glow

    Illumes each sojourner. Him with deep roar

        Fierce lions fled, with fear distraught,

        At spells, that o'er the deep he brought.

    Phoebus, the nation's founder, bade

The monsters cower dismayed ;
Lest aught should fail of all his word, Once plighted to Cyrene's lord.

STROPHE.

Remedies for every ill
    To mortal men and dames the God imparts ;
And gave the lyre ; and grants the muse at will.
        He in men's hearts
    Plants Order fair, whom Discord flees ;
        And reigns in his prophetic shrine.
        Thus he in Sparta, and divine
Pylos, and Argos, bade the heroes dwell
    Born of Aegimius and Heracles.
From Sparta springs my own ancestral boast, as legends tell.

ANTISTROPHE.

Sprung from thence, to Thera's land,
    Heroes of Aegid stock, my fathers came,   70
Unaided not of Heaven ; Fate's guiding hand
        Conveyed the flame
    Of festal sacrifice, (whence we
        Have learnt, Apollo, to thy state
        Carneia's feast to celebrate,)
E'en to Cyrene's city proudly placed,
    Home of the mail-clad Antenoridae,
From Troy that came with Helen, when their fatherland lay waste

EPODE.

In war. And that chivalrous band to greet
 With sacrifice, forth came—and presents gave—   80
The folk that Battus brought ; when with swift fleet
  A path he opened o'er the deep sea wave,
   And wider sanctuaries made,
   And straight across the champaign laid
  The rock-paved road, hoof-trampled by the train
  Of Him that shields from pain,—
Apollo. There, behind the mart, Entombed the Founder lies apart.

STROPHE.

Erst with men he sojourned blest,
 Whom as a hero now his folk adore.
Apart—the tomb their portion—others rest,   90
   Great kings, before
  The palace : their achievements high
   Besprinkled all with dews of song
   Soft streaming from the festal throng.
These, lapt in earth, the tale of bliss partake
 And share their kinsman's well-won victory ;
Who now Youth's song to Phoebus of the golden lyre must wake,

ANTISTROPHE.

Pytho's noble strain repays
 His contest's lavished cost, melodious chant

Of victory. The wise resound his praise ;   100
      'Tis but the vaunt
   Of all I utter ! Mind and tongue
     Are his of force beyond his years ;
     Bold,—as an eagle, he appears,
Mid humbler fowls spreading his pinions wide ;
   And, as a fortress, in the lists is strong ;
From childhood, high he soared in Song ; his skill the car-race tried.

EPODE.

Bold hath he trod each path of local praise,
   With might made perfect now by Heaven's goodwill,
And, O blest Cronidae ! in after days   110
   Such might, in act and counsel, grant him still.
     Lest wintry blasts, that breathe decay,
     Should sweep the fruits of time away.
   With guiding favour Zeus attends
   The fortunes of His friends :
Oh, in Olympia e'en such grace May He bestow on Battus' race !

PYTHIAN VI.

*TO XENOCRATES OF ACRAGAS, VICTOR IN THE CHARIOT-RACE;
A BROTHER OF THERO, TO WHOM OLYMP. II. IS DEDICATED.*

STROPHE.

OH list! for or in lands where glancing-eyed
      Aphrodite reigns,
      Or Graces fair, we plough the plains :
And to Earth's resonant centre ride.
    Where songs of favoured Emmenids that tell,
      And Acragas, and thee, Xenocrates,
      Songs for Pythian victories,
Lie, meetly stored, With the golden hoard
    That fills Apollo's rampired dell !

ANTISTROPHE.

And never shall the rain-cloud's mustered host   10
      Roaring fierce and deep,
      Nor furious winds that treasure sweep
To Ocean's cells, mid shingle tost
    And battered. No ! in clear light see it shine ;

And to thy sire, O Thrasybulus, bear
Triumph, all thy house may share ;
While spreads the tale, How in Crisa's vale
The victor-chariot's boast was thine !

STROPHE.

That mandate thou at thy right hand hast set
Cleaving to it still,   20
That erst upon his native hill
Would Philyra's son ('tis said) repeat
To young Achilles, of his parents left :
How "most to Zeus, the pealing thunder's king,
"Loyal service man should bring ;
"Nor filial care From a parent e'er,
"Through all his portioned years, be reft."

ANTISTROPHE.

Such mind Antilochus in byegone day,
Dauntless warrior, bare :
Who for a father death did dare,   30
And stood in Memnon's murderous way,
Fell Aethiop chief ! For, smit with Paris' dart,
A horse checked Nestor's chariot ; and the foe
'Gan his heavy spear to throw,
And cries dismayed To his son for aid
Burst from the old Messenian's heart.

STROPHE.

Nor wasted on the earth his words he flung :
    Firm the hero stood,
    And for his father gave his blood.
Thus in his day to all the young
    Seemed that achiever of a deed of might
      Pattern most fair of filial bravery.
      All of this is now gone by,
But Thrasybule By the ancient rule
    Walks most of later men aright.

ANTISTROPHE.

And treads his uncle's paths, his worth revealed !
    Wealth he well doth guide,
    Nor stains Youth's flower with sin or pride ;
But culls all lore the Muses yield ;
    And, joying in equestrian strife, to Thee,
      Shaker of earth, Poseidon ! pleased doth bend,
      Kind of heart, and such a friend
To all that share In his feasts, as ne'er
    So sweet was fretwork of the bee !

PYTHIAN VII.

TO MEGACLES OF ATHENS (A MEMBER OF THE FAMOUS ALCMAEONID FAMILY), VICTOR IN THE CHARIOT-RACE.

STROPHE.

BE glorious Athens our prelude meet!
Fair key-stone she, for songs that greet
　　Alcmaeon's mighty seed,
　　Praising their coursers' speed!
For never country I shall name,
And never house, whose fame
　　Than these hath rung more clear
　　In every Grecian ear.

ANTISTROPHE.

Ay, sounded are they through all the lands,—
Those labours of Erecthid hands,　　　　　　　　　10
　　On Pytno's steep divine
　　Rearing Apollo's shrine!
Five Isthmian victories claim my lays,
And one surpassing praise

Gained by Olympia's fane,
And yet—in Cirrha—twain !

EPODE.

Such, Megacles, thy fathers' deeds and thine !
I welcome this last feat ; and but repine,
    That envy aye entangles deeds so fair.
Well ! the old tale is true :—when Heaven would bless   20
Man's hopes with blooms of lasting happiness,
    Evil still mingles there !

PYTHIAN VIII.

TO ARISTOMENES OF AEGINA, VICTOR IN THE BOYS'
WRESTLING-MATCH.

STROPHE.

O DAUGHTER kind—Tranquillity—
    Of Justice ! making cities great !
    Alike of battle and debate
The keys supreme are held of thee.
    Take from Aristomenes this Pythian triumph-chant !
For well thou know'st, in season meet, The mutual dues of friendship sweet
    Now to win, and now to grant.

ANTISTROPHE.

But thou, whene'er in human breast
    Rankles the sting of ruthless spite,
    Uprising in thy wrath, the might   10
Of those fierce foemen combatest,

Whelming in the deep their rage. Porphyrion thus did rouse
Thine ire, nor knew how mad his sin ! But choicest is the gain we win
From a willing giver's house.

EPODE.

The haughtiest in time hath their own rage destroyed.
Not hundred-headed Typho might such doom avoid ;
No, nor the Giants' King ! They fell by lightnings slain
And shafts of that Apollo, who now in love receives
Xenarces' son, as crowned with proud Parnassian leaves
From Cirrha home he brings the Doric revel-train !   20

STROPHE.

Not banished from the Graces lies
His home, in all the virtues rare
Of Aeäcids that claimeth share.
No ! from that righteous island's rise
Never-failing praise is hers, and songs her worth proclaim.
Oft have the heroes she has borne The crown of sportive contests worn,
Oft in rapid fight won fame.

ANTISTROPHE.

Brave mortal sons she boasts beside ;
But time would fail, or e'er should I

In harping and sweet melody   30
  Shrine the long tale of all her pride ;
    Cloying surfeit thence would spring,—but *this*, at hand that lies.
Thy feat, young hero! may my craft On swiftest pinions skyward waft,
    Latest deed of fair emprise !

EPODE.

Thou with thy mother's brethren keep'st as wrestler pace,
Nor Theognetus in Olympia dost disgrace,
  Nor bold Clitomachus, the Isthmian meed that won !
Midylus' house thou raisest, and such renown is thine,
As, gazing on the foe with spears in stubborn line,
  In seven-gated Thebes spake, riddling, Oecles' son.   40

STROPHE.

When in the foot-steps of their sires
  From Argos came the Epigoni,
  Above the battle rose his cry :
"Tis Nature's power yon valour fires
  " Passing on from sire to son. E'en now, with clearest sight,
" Foremost I view Alcmaeon shake In Cadmus' gates the pictured snake
  " Flashing on his buckler bright.

ANTISTROPHE.

"And he, that erst was overcome,

    "Now 'neath the gracious influence lies

    "Of fairer-boding auguries,   50

"The brave Adrastus. Yet his home

    "Soon an adverse doom must rue. For of all Greeks alone,

"So Heaven ordains, he home shall bring His hosts unharmed, (yet gathering

    "Ashes of a slaughtered son,)

EPODE.

"To Abas' wide-wayed town!" Such utterance the seer

Amphiaraus poured. And thus with gladsome cheer

    Alcmaeon I will deck with wreaths, and sprinkled lays,

For He, my Spirit-neighbour, safeguard of all that's mine,

Before me, as I fared to Earth's famed central shrine,

    Appearing told Heaven's will in heirloom prophet-ways!   60

STROPHE.

O launcher of the rapid dart,

    Lord of the hospitable cell

    Whose fame illumines Pytho's dell,

There to our friend didst thou impart

    That supreme success, and in his home hadst given before

(At feasts of thee and Artemis) The five-fold contest's meed of bliss.

    Now in love, I thee implore,

ANTISTROPHE.

Look down ; while in melodious song
  Each theme of triumph I pursue !
  Protecting Justice stands, 'tis true,   70
To bless our tuneful revel-throng :
  Yet, Xenarces, for thy house I'll ask Heaven's favour still.
For though the many's praise he gains, That wins success by slightest
      pains,
  Though he seems by prescient skill—

EPODE.

Wise in an unwise world—to rear his high estate :
With man such issues rest not—all is sent of Fate !
  And now she lifts us high, and now her hands in turn
Crush us to earth ! Well, thine is Megara's meed, and thine
The prize of Marathon, and thou with triumphs trine
  In Hera's local games success by toil didst earn.   80

STROPHE.

On rivals four swooped from on high
  With purpose dire thy fierce attack !
  To them a joyous journey back
Did Pytho's stern award deny,
  Them no mother's smiling welcome, home returned, might bless.
Shrinking through by-ways dark they go, And shun abashed each jeer-
      ing foe,
  Wounded sore with sharp distress.

ANTISTROPHE.

But who in tender youth hath gained
    The praise of recent victory
    Kindles with expectation high   90
And soars on valour's wings sustained :
    Nobler quest than wealth is his ! Full soon to greatness grow
The boons that gladden mortals' state, Yet fall to earth as soon, when
        Fate,
    Adverse, wills their overthrow.

EPODE.

What are we, great or lowly ?   Creatures of a day !
Man 's but a phantom dream.   Yet, in the gracious ray
    Poured from on high, his life puts joy and glory on.
Aegina, gentle mother, in courses free and fair,
With Zeus and Aeäcus, this city onwards bear,
    With Peleus brave, Achilles eke, and Telamon !   100

PYTHIAN IX.

TO TELESICRATES OF CYRENE, VICTOR IN THE RACE IN FULL ARMOUR.

STROPHE.

WITH the deep-zoned Graces fain am I
  To chant the victor from Pytho's field,
  Telesicrates, lord of the brazen shield,
Blest hero, pride of great Cyrene's chivalry !
Cyrene, that Leto's son of yore From breezy hollows of Pelion bore,—
Huntress-maid,—in his car of gold, And gave rich realms to her
      queenly hold ;
  With many a fruitful field, and many a herd,
  A fair domain to rule, the mainland's blooming third.

ANTISTROPHE.

And the silver-sandalled Queen of Love
  The stranger Delian welcome made,   10
  O'er the heavenly car as her light touch played ;
And modest grace she spread their blissful couch above,
Close linking in love her Guest divine With that fair daughter of
      Hypseus' line—

Monarch he of the Lapithae, From Ocean sprung in the next degree,
  Whom in famed Pindus' dales Creusa bare,
  The Sea-nymph, erst that joyed Peneüs' couch to share,

EPODE.

  Daughter of Earth ; and Hypseus reared
Cyrene fair.   Small joy she found To guide the shuttle's tortuous
      round,
  Or share the feasts, her home-pent mates that cheered !
    But brazen javelins she threw,   20
    And savage beasts with brandished falchion slew,
  Making in restful peace to dwell
The cattle of her sire, and yielding scanty space
To Slumber's sweet embrace,
  When on her weary eyes at dawn he fell.

STROPHE.

  As unarmed, unaided, she defied
    And grappled fearless a lion fierce,
    Came Apollo, with arrows afar that pierce,
  And straight from out his halls called Chiron to his side.
" Come, Philyra's son, and quit thy cave, And gazing marvel how
      strong and brave   30
" She that fearlessly thus contends ; A maid, whose mettle all toil
      transcends ;

" With calm resolve, untossed by gusts of dread !
" What mortal gave her birth ? Of what high lineage bred

ANTISTROPHE.

" Doth she roam the mountains' caves of gloom,
  "And joy in might that no bounds confine?
  " Shall I stay not, but seize her in grasp divine ;
" Or bide the wedding couch, and cull the honeyed bloom ? "
And answer the mighty Centaur made, While tranquil smiles on his
          calm brow played,
" Modest wooing unlocks," quoth he, " Divine love's treasures with
      secret key
  " 'Mid Gods and mortals both Shame holds her sway,   40
  " And love's first raptures shrink abashed from sight of day.

EPODE.

" Sure, for from thee all falsehood flies,
" Some sportive mood thy speech inspired ! Hast *thou* yon maiden's
      race inquired,
  " O King ? that know'st the final destinies
      " And paths of each created thing.
      " What leaves from earth outburst in days of spring,
  " What sands are tost in sea or rill
" By waves or eddying winds, and what must needs befall,
" And whence,—thou knowest all !
      " Yet, forced by Wisdom's challenge, speak I will !   50

STROPHE.

" To this glen, to wed yon maiden, thou
    "Art come ; and with her across the sea,
    " To the glorious garden of Zeus shalt flee,
" There make her queen, and round the hill's plain-cinctured brow
" Draw to her an island-folk. For sake Of thee, shall Libya welcome
                make
" Yon fair maiden, with her to reign, In golden halls, o'er the spacious
                plain ;
    " And bid her share the queenship of the place ;
    " Nor aught of fruitful plants withhold, nor beasts of chase.

ANTISTROPHE.

" She shall bear a son, whom Hermes great
    " Shall from her loving embrace away   60
    " To the fair-thronèd Hours and to Earth convey ;
    " And they upon their knees the favoured babe shall seat,
" And rain on his lips ambrosial dews, That deathless life shall in
                him infuse,
" E'en as Zeus or Apollo fair A joy to mortals,—their flocks his
                care,—
    " And Agreus, Nomius, Aristaeus hight !"
He spake, and bade fulfil the wedlock's joyous rite.

EPODE.

The Gods full swiftly win their aims,
Short are their paths :—that day wrought all ! They met in Libya's
    golden hall :
    Where, o'er a glorious city,—and in games
      Renowned, she fixes yet her seat.   70
      And her thy son, Carneades ! did greet
  With bliss but now in Pytho earned.
The nymph his triumph shared, and welcomes him again
Victor from Pytho's fane
  To his own land of lovely dames returned.

STROPHE.

But the praise of noble worth flows free ;
    In themes so boundless choice words and few
    Win the ear of the prudent, and Measure due
In all holds sway supreme. Great Iolaus, thee
No scorner of Measure Thebes did own ! Eurystheus fell by thy
    sword o'erthrown ;   80
Thee they laid by thy grandsire's grave, That swiftly of yore his
  coursers drave,
  Amphitryon, welcomed by the Dragon's Seed
  To Cadmus' city thronged with many a milk-white steed.

ANTISTROPHE.

At a single birth twin issue sprung
    To him and Zeus, from Alcmena wise,
    That in valour surpassed, and in victories.
Dull are the lips that leave great Heracles unsung,
Or e'er can forget how Dirce's wave To him and Iphicles nurture
    gave !
Songs of triumph to them I'll bear, That with fulfilment have crowned
    my prayer.
    Sweet Graces, may your light attend me still !   90
    For at Aegina he, and thrice on Nisus' hill,

EPODE.

    From tongue-tied shame this town did free.
Such strivings for his townsmen's weal Let neither foe nor friend
    conceal,
    Nor slight the ancient prophet of the sea,
        Who bade mankind full praise bestow
        E'en on the prowess of a noble foe !
    Full oft upon thy victories,
At Pallas' yearly feasts, hath gazed each wondering maid,
And silently hath prayed
    For spouse or son like Telesicrates.   100

STROPHE.

At Olympia eke, and in the games
   Of Earth deep-bosomed, and far and wide
   Through the land of his, dwelling! A tale of pride
The thirst I fain would quench awakes anew, and claims
Meet lays for his noble sires of old, That seeking Irasa's distant hold
Wooed a Libyan maiden rare, Antaeus' daughter with radiant hair ;
   Whom many a kinsman lord of high degree,
   And many a stranger sought, for fair of form was she !

ANTISTROPHE.

And afire were all to bear away
   Her golden-coronalled youth's fair fruit.   110
   But her father had purposed a nobler suit.
For Danaus' tale he knew,—how, ere might life's mid day
His forty and eight fair maids o'ertake, A speedy spousal the sire did
         make :
All at once did the virgin band In Argos' lists at the race-goal stand
   Then, as in speed suitor with suitor vied,
   At Danaus' bidding each won with his prize a bride !

EPODE.

His daughter's spouse the Libyan found
E'en thus. In rich array her place Hard by the goal she took, the race
   To guerdon ; and her sire proclaimed around,

Who clasped her first, should claim the prize.   120
 Swift o'er the course Alexidamus flies,
And seized her hand in his, and bore
His bride through nomad hosts of horsemen, raining down
Full many a leaf and crown,
 And many a triumph-plume was his before.

PYTHIAN X.

TO HIPPOCLES OF PELINNAEUM IN SICILY, VICTOR IN THE BOYS' DOUBLE FOOT-RACE.

STROPHE.

O SPARTA, bliss is thine,

And blest is Thessaly ! In either land, the line

    Of one unvanquished sire, Alcides' children reign.

Boast I untimely ? Nay, for Pelinnaeum calls aloud

And Pytho, and Aleuas' sons : applauses proud

    For Hippocles they claim from all the festal train.

ANTISTROPHE.

For lo ! he tastes the games ;

While, to the nations round, Parnassus' vale proclaims,

    How, o'er her two-fold course, first of the youths he sped.

In joy, O Phoebus, opes and ends each task by Heaven begun ; 10

'Tis by thy counsels led, this exploit he hath done,

    By kindred glories fired his father's paths to tread !

EPODE.

In strife-sustaining arms that father triumphs twain

Did at Olympia gain :

And, where steep Cirrha soars above the fertile mead,

To Phricias fell anew the prize of speed.
May Fortune, constant still, in coming hours,
Adorn their wealthy house with triumph's radiant flowers.

STROPHE.

In Greece no scanty share
Of all her joys they won : oh, may Heaven's envy ne'er   20
    Bring dark reverse, be hearts divine void still of spite !
Blest in his lot is he, and crowned with hymns of all the wise,
With prowess of strong arm or nimble foot, the prize
    Of strife supreme that wins, by daring both, and might ;

ANTISTROPHE.

And, more, that lives to gaze
Thus on a son adorned duly with Pytho's bays !
    What though the brazen heights of heaven he may not scale ?
Yet of all joys that man may taste, his voyage hath reached the goal,
Albeit to the tribes that dwell beyond the pole,
    To find the wondrous path, nor fleets nor feet avail !   30

EPODE.

For princely Perseus these the banquet spread of yore ;
Who passed their palace door,
And met them, as they slew, to grace Apollo's rites,
Proud hecatombs of asses.   Still delights
The God in these their holy hymns and feasts,
Viewing with smile serene the rearing uncouth beasts.

STROPHE.

Nor at their customs stands
The Muse aloof, but all around the maiden bands
    Dance ever to the sound of harp and shrilling fife ;
Their locks with golden laurel crowned, they feast in careless joy. 40
Disease nor wasting eld may e'er their bliss alloy.
    A consecrated race, remote from toil and strife,

ANTISTROPHE.

They dwell, from vengeance free
Of jealous Fortune. There the son of Danae
    In flush of hardihood came by Athene led
To those blest companies. 'Twas he the Gorgon slew, and bare
Back to his island-folk a stony Death, with hair
    Of writhing serpents crowned, the monster's glittering head.

EPODE.

Mine be it, ne'er at feats that heavenly Powers achieve
To marvel, but believe !   50
Stay, Muse, the oar ; and cast the anchor from the prow,
Fixed for defence against the reefs below !
From theme to theme, the bright applausive lay,
As bees from flower to flower, speeds on its changeful way.

STROPHE.

While my sweet music's sound
The Ephyraeans raise Peneus' streams around ;

Fain would I lift thy praise, Hippocles, higher yet,
And bid thy peers and elders both these triumph-crowns admire,
And make thee dear to all the gentle maiden quire,
    Thus divers passions aye 'neath divers bosoms fret.   60

ANTISTROPHE.

Whate'er his aim, let each
Soon as he wins it, clasp the bliss within his reach :
    For what a year may bring no prescience can prove.
In friendly Thorax rests my trust, who, toiling for my grace,
Hath yoked this car of song with steeds in fourfold trace,
    And gives me guidance back for guidance, love for love.

EPODE.

Gold, and the upright soul, on the assaying stone
Are to the tester shown !
His noble brothers too with him we celebrate,
Who lift to heights of fame Thessalia's state.   70
Thus ever in a worthy ruler's hand
The guidance lies, aright that steers a fatherland.

PYTHIAN XI.

TO THRASYDAEUS OF THEBES, VICTOR IN THE BOYS'
FOOT-RACE.

STROPHE.

MAY Cadmus' daughters, Semele 'mid heavenly queens that dwells,
And Ino, fair Leucothea, that shares the Nereids' cells,
    And she that bare Alcides, matchless boast !
Speed, where the golden tripods lie In Melia's hallowed treasury,
    The shrine, that aye of all hath Loxias honoured most.

ANTISTROPHE.

Ismenium he named it, home of truth, the prophets' seat.
And there, Harmonia's children, now, in serried bands to meet,
    Your nation's heroine hosts Apollo calls !
To sing of Themis, queen divine, And Earth's prophetic central shrine,
    And Pytho, while around the lingering twilight falls.   10

EPODE.

Of Thebes' seven-gated town,
    And Cirrha's lists they sing,
    Where, waking memories fair, did Thrasydaeus fling
On his ancestral hearth a third triumphal crown,

Won in rich lands, where Pylades of old—
Spartan Orestes' friend—his sway did hold.

STROPHE.

Orestes, whom Arsinoë preserved from mischief dire,
When 'neath the forceful hands of Clytemnaestra fell his sire,
   And Priam's daughter eke—Dardanian maid—
Cassandra, she with falchion hoar Sped forth, to tread the forest
    shore   20
   Of gloomy Acheron with Agamemnon's shade.

ANTISTROPHE.

Relentless queen! Or sprang such rage from thoughts of her that
    died,
Iphigeneia, far away by swift Euripus' side?
   Or did she to a lawless passion yield,
Lured to an alien's dark embrace? Oh deed most foul, that heaps
    disgrace
   On youthful brides, nor art its stain hath e'er concealed!

EPODE.

Strangers her shame resound,
   And townsmen join the cry!
   Proportioned envy still attends prosperity,
And censure's murmur breathes unmarked along the ground.   30
   So fell the hero son of Atreus slain,
   To famed Amyclae home returned again.

STROPHE.

And with him fell the prophet-maid, when Troy's proud halls in flame
He low had laid for Helen's sake. And so Orestes came
    To ancient Strophius' care, that dwelt beneath
Parnassus' spurs. Yet, childhood past, His tardy vengeance smote at
      last
    The guilty dame, and bade Aegisthus share her death.

ANTISTROPHE.

Thus, or where devious cross the paths of song, O friends, I stray
From that straight course, that erst I held; or from my purposed way
    Such winds as toss the sea-skiffs me have flung!   40
Yet, Muse, since thou for silver fee To venal utterance didst agree,
    'Tis thine on various themes to ply the vagrant tongue!

EPODE.

And now the victor sire,
    And now the son we praise,
    Whose bliss and glory, blent in growing splendour, blaze.
First where Olympia's lists the copious hymn inspire,
    Flushed with fair triumph in the chariot-race,
    They with their steeds shared fame that spreads apace:

STROPHE.

To Pytho's naked stadium descending next they strove
With Hellas' hosts in speed. Be mine the boons of Heaven to love, 50
                    K

Within my powers shaping my manhood's aim !
The modest mean I still have found With choicest blessings wreathed
    around
    In all the city : thus the despot's lot I blame,

ANTISTROPHE.

And on would press to triumphs free for all ! For baleful spite
Recoils from him, with calm restraint that rules his fortune's height,
    And shuns pride's surfeit. Thus to darksome death
With fairer ending he shall come, And to the dear ones of his home
    —That best of all good gifts—an honoured name bequeath.

EPODE.

The son of Iphicles,
    Thus, 'mid applausive song,   60
    To greatness Iolaus grew : and Castor strong,
And Polydeuces, sovereign seed of Deities,
    From day to day that trod alternate, now
    Therapnae's halls, and now Olympus' brow !

PYTHIAN XII.

TO MIDAS OF ACRAGAS, WINNER OF THE PRIZE FOR FLUTE-PLAYING.

STROPHE.

I PRAY thee, Queen of splendour; city of peerless grace ;
Persephone's home ; O thou, that on thy tower-clad hill
   Dwellest, fair Queen, beside the streams of pastoral Acragas !
Propitious greet, with favour of Heaven and man's goodwill,
The crown, at Pytho's festival that glorious Midas won ;
   And welcome him, victorious in that fair art,—of old
   That Pallas found, when wailed the Gorgons bold,
And she to music wove their dismal moan.

ANTISTROPHE.

For maiden-shrieks and hiss of horrible snakes she heard,
Forth flowing in plaintive strain with weary anguish fraught ;   10
   What time as Perseus did to death that sister-triad's third,
And ruin to the hosts of Seriphos' island brought ;
And blindness therewithal he poured on Phorcus' immortal race ;
   And Polydectes rued the gift, the son of Danae gave
   To him, perforce that made her wife and slave ;
When headless lay Medusa, fair of face,

STROPHE.

Slain by the hero, sprung, they say, from a golden rain !
But, when from his peril she had saved her champion dear,
    Maiden Athene fashioned then the flute with its varied strain,
To echo back the wailing that smote upon her ear,   20
As clamorously forth from fell Euryale's maw it came.
    So found the goddess,—and forthwith on mortal man bestowed,
    And named the strain her " many-headed mode ; "
Memorial fair of each frequented game !

ANTISTROPHE.

Through slender brass it flows ; through many a reeden quill,
That grew by the Graces' town for choral dance renowned,
    In nymph Cephisis' hallowed haunts ; true witness of dancers'
        skill !
Ne'er, save by toiling, mortal hath aught of blessing found ;
But all that lacks, in one brief day, can Destiny's power supply.
    What fate ordains may none avoid : needs must a day befall   30
    Of chances unforeseen, that, maugre all
Man's scheming, part will grant and part deny !